Su

Suppressed
By
Wendi L. Wilson

Wendi L. Wilson

Suppressed

Copyright ©2017 by Wendi L. Wilson

All rights reserved. No part of this book may be reproduced, transmitted, downloaded, or distributed, or stored in a retrieval system, or transmitted in any form or by any means, without express permission of the author, except by a reviewer who my quote brief passages for review purposes.

This is a work of fiction. Names, characters, organizations, places, events, and incidents are either products of the author's imagination or used fictitiously. Any resemblance to actual persons, living or dead, or actual events is purely coincidental.

Cover Design by Molly Phipps

www.wegotyoucoveredbookdesign.com

Wendi L. Wilson

Suppressed

For Alisa, who told me I could do it and made me believe it. I will be eternally grateful.

Wendi L. Wilson

Suppressed

Chapter 1

"I'm done."

"What do you mean, you're done? You'll get back to work right now, or so help me, I'll make you regret it, Princess."

"I told you not to call me that, you old hag! I'm leaving, and there's nothing you can do about it. Clean this crappy house yourself."

"Kailani!"

"What?"

I'm ripped from another daydream by my mother's urgent voice. I'm disappointed because this time I was really letting Ms. Coraline have it. My body is on autopilot as I start mechanically rubbing the mirror with the soft cloth in my hand. I try to retreat back into the fantasy because I'm pretty sure I was going to slap the old lady just before I walked out the door.

"You should have finished this room an hour ago," my mother says in a quiet voice.

I give up on continuing my glorious dream exit and turn to look at mom. Her bright red hair is tied up with a blue bandana, and she has dirt smudged on her nose. The urgency in the green depths of her eyes makes me want to roll mine, but I somehow manage to refrain.

"Mom, she's not even here. I'll be done before she gets back."

"Just go, Kai. I'll finish here." She smooths my hair, tucking a lock as vibrant as her own behind my ear with a smile. "It's almost time for school. You should go get ready."

I take a look at the watch on my arm, a large masculine piece, the only thing I have of a father I've never met. He left us when I was a baby. I don't know why I treasure a watch from a man who couldn't be bothered to stick around for me, but I do.

The hands tell me it's nearly eight. I've been cleaning for two and a half hours, trying to take some of the workload off mom. She's been looking tired lately, so I've been doubling up on my chores. I don't know why Ms. Coraline works her so hard, or why my mom stays. She refuses to talk about it, only saying that this is where we have to be.

Suppressed

I rush up the spiral staircase to my room, all the way up to the third floor of the spacious mansion. I pull the rubber band from my hair as I walk, shaking the red tresses free while trying to finger comb out the tangles. Once in my room, I pull off my dirty work clothes and cross the space to my closet. It only takes ten steps to get there. The room is barely big enough to hold my twin bed and a dresser, but it's mine. My only refuge in this place from the old hag who owns it.

I snatch a pair of jeans and a faded flannel shirt from the closet and walk quickly across the hall to the small bathroom my mother and I share. After washing my face and brushing my teeth, I get dressed and head back to my room for my shoes and backpack. Another glance at my watch tells me that if I hurry I'll have enough time to swing by the kitchen for a bagel before I need to leave. I slip on a pair of dock shoes with no socks and grab my bag.

I screech to a halt halfway down the stairs, nearly losing my balance and toppling the rest of the way, when I hear it. It's the one thing guaranteed to dampen my spirits and ruin my day. It's the dreaded voice of Ms. Coraline.

"Why isn't this room finished? I expected it to be one hundred percent spotless by the time I returned."

"I'm sorry, ma'am."

I grit my teeth at my mother's words. Oh, how I hate when she calls that old hag ma'am. I tiptoe my way down the rest of the steps, silently thanking God for the carpet runner that muffles my footsteps. I decide to forgo breakfast, for the path to the kitchen leads right by the parlor where my mom is pandering to that hateful old lady she calls boss.

I slip through the front door and close it with a soft click behind me. Swinging my backpack over my shoulder, I run down the driveway as fast as my legs will take me… which isn't really that fast. I am, by no stretch of the imagination, a runner. My legs are better equipped for the water. I inhale deeply at the thought of water, breathing in the briny breeze blowing from the back of the house.

The house's proximity to the sea is the only, and I mean only, positive thing about living with Ms. Coraline. A set of rickety wood steps leads from the back veranda straight down to the beach. The small window in my bedroom overlooks it. I can swim whenever I want, which is pretty much every day. It's my escape when the confines of my room close in on me.

A large truck rattles by, pulling me from my reverie. I slow my steps, watching the bright white and orange cargo vehicle slow down as it passes me. I get a little nervous because, well, I'm alone, on a private road, and it's a cargo truck. This is every would-be kidnapper's dream. I stop and pick up a jagged rock just to be safe.

The tension leaves my body as the truck turns right and slowly drives out of sight. I release the rock and stare at the red marks on my palm where the serrated edges cut into the flesh. I shake out my hand, wipe it on the leg of my jeans and start walking again. As I reach the drive where the truck turned, I notice the word "sold" printed in bright red letters on the faded real estate sign.

Someone bought the old McCormick place. The thought rolls through my brain as I walk the rest of the way to school. It feels weird having neighbors. Mr. McCormick lived all alone in that huge house for most of my childhood. He died when I was ten, and the house sat empty the last six years while wrapped up in probate. I wonder what the new people will be like. Ms. Coraline hated old Mr. McCormick so I never actually met him. Of course, she hates everyone, so she'll probably forbid me from talking to the new people too.

The high school comes into view and I break into a jog, knowing it's useless. Thanks to my slow, thoughtful pace, I'm late. I walk through the doors of the L-shaped, one story building and head straight for the office. Santa Lorelei High services the entire island, which has a population of only about two thousand. The entire high school houses only about a hundred and twenty-five students at any given time, so there's no way I can sneak into my homeroom class unnoticed. I gave up trying two years ago.

"Miss Ericson. So nice of you to join us."

The receptionist in the main office speaks to me in a pleasant voice, just as she always does. It doesn't matter when I arrive, she is always kind. I'm sure she knows Ms. Coraline, knows what I have to deal with every day and takes it easy on me out of pity. Whatever. I'll take it.

"Sorry, Mrs. White," I mumble.

Suppressed

"It's quite all right, dear," the older lady tells me. "You're actually just in time to do me a favor."

I raise one eyebrow, wondering what I could possibly do for her. She smiles, then nods her head as her eyes focus on something behind me. I take a quick peek over my shoulder to see what she's looking at. At least, I mean for it to be a quick peek. There's a boy I've never seen before sitting against the wall. As I turn, I catch him staring at my butt before his eyes quickly rise to meet mine.

I'm sure my face is a glowing red sea, my freckles standing out like tiny islands. I quickly forget the embarrassment, however, when he continues to stare without speaking. His eyes are a deep blue, like the ocean in my backyard, and I can't seem to look away as a calm settles over me.

"Kailani, this is Bryce Howell," Mrs. White says, breaking me out of my trance. I turn toward her as she continues. "Today is his first day, and I would like you to show him around."

I open my mouth to object, but a stern look from Mrs. White has me snapping it shut again. I hate being the center of attention and walking into class with a hot new guy is going to put me right into the fire. I frown at the thought. Hot? I turn and take another look at him. At least this time he's looking at Mrs. White, not my butt.

His dark hair is sticking out at weird angles and, as I watch, he runs his fingers through it showing me the cause of its disarray. His face is smooth and clear, not sporting that day-old stubble most junior boys have, trying look sexy but failing. He is wearing faded blue jeans and a white t-shirt, which doesn't leave much to the imagination. Is he hot? Why, yes. Yes, he is.

A smirk turns up one side of his mouth as his eyes turn toward me and he catches me staring. I quickly turn back to face Mrs. White, feeling my face heat up again.

Gah, having pale skin and freckles is so annoying. I couldn't hide a blush if my life depended on it.

I shoot her a pleading look, but she ignores it, saying, "Thank you, Miss Ericson. I'll excuse your tardy. You two better be on your way." And just like that, we're dismissed.

Taking a deep breath and letting it out slowly, I turn to face him. He unfolds his frame from the chair, stretching as he stands. My eyes are drawn to a sliver of bare skin exposed between his shirt and belt as he bends slightly backwards during his stretch.

"Ahem."

My eyes snap to his, and he smiles that cocky boy smile I've seen so many times in this school. The I-know-I'm-hot smile. I hate that smile. But on this boy, it's…I don't know. It has a ring of truth I can't deny. Then, he opens his mouth.

"My eyes are up here."

I blush for the third time in five minutes, but my embarrassment quickly turns to righteous indignation. I'd seriously just caught him ogling my behind, and he's calling me out for taking a peek at his abs? What a jerk.

I push through the door, not waiting to see if he'll follow. If he gets lost, it's his problem, not mine. I shake my head at the thought. Nobody could get lost in this tiny school. If I hurry, I may be able to slip into homeroom before him and people won't assume we're together. I quicken my pace.

I reach the door and make to grab the handle, but instead of smooth metal, my hand closes around warm flesh. I jerk it back as if burned and see a hand with long, well-manicured fingers already wrapped around the knob. A voice close to my ear startles me.

"If you wanted to hold hands, you should have told me," he says.

The mockery in his voice is evident. I grit my teeth and step back, allowing him to open the door. He motions for me to precede him and I do, walking quickly with my head down, eyes on the floor. I drop my tardy pass on the teacher's desk and stride to my normal seat in the back.

"Class, we have a new student," Mr. Jonas says, but I refuse to look up. I can't stand the thought of those eyes mocking me again.

"This is Bryce Howell. Tell us a bit about yourself, Mr. Howell."

You could hear a pin drop, everyone was so focused on Bryce. We don't get many new students here. In fact, the last one was my friend Ana Fuentes, who moved here in second grade. The whole class is riveted. I sneak a glance around and see most of the girls in the class leaning forward in their seats, waiting for him to speak.

Suppressed

"Hi," Bryce says. "I'm Bryce, and I just moved here from California. I am an only child, and I like long walks on the beach."

A smattering of giggles erupts in the class. The girls are eating this crap up. I roll my eyes in disgust, only to see Bryce staring at me again. He smirks and heads to an empty seat in the front row.

"Thank you, Mr. Howell. That was...enlightening." Mr. Jonas shakes his head. He doesn't like this guy any more than I do. "All right class, homeroom is over, so open your math books to page seventy-eight."

Out of the corner of my eye I see Bryce look around in confusion. I smile, knowing he's probably wondering why we aren't moving to a new class with new students, the way most high schools do. Santa Lorelei has only twenty-eight kids in the junior class, so we all have the same classes together. All day. Every day.

I see him shrug and tap Sandy Evans on the shoulder before whispering into her ear. She giggles. What is it with the giggling today? Bryce scoots his chair next to hers and puts his arm around her back so he can lean in to see her book.

It's disgusting, the way she starts tittering and preening. I feel like I could vomit.

It's the same the rest of the morning. We move to our next class, which is chemistry, in the science lab down the hall. There's no need for Mrs. Gardner to introduce him, so we put on our safety goggles and light our Bunsen burners. I glance around the room and spot Bryce, this time next to Amelia Boggs. He's half standing, half sitting on the stool, whispering something, his mouth close to her ear. She doesn't giggle, I'll give her that. She is smiling at him though, a seductive curve of the lips as if she has a secret she'd like to tell only him.

The stool next to me is empty. Ana is my lab partner, but she's absent today. I could really use her sarcastic wit right now. She'd be tearing these girls to shreds for their simpering antics. My lip curls with the thought. I can't wait to hear what she'll say about this.

I feel eyes on me and glance around. In their turn about the room, my eyes are snagged once again by the dark blue depths of Bryce's. For some reason, I can't look away. Then he smiles. It's a sardonic smile, one full of challenge. Two can play this game so I continue to stare, refusing to be the

Suppressed

first to fold. His smile grows bigger, showing a row of bright white teeth. My face grows hot, once again, as I stare at him.

I don't know what it is about this guy. I've blushed more this morning than I have in the last six months. Suddenly, his eyes flit away, and I realize that Mrs. Gardner has called his name. Looking back at my chemistry notes, I smile and mentally pat myself on the back. It feels like a victory, staring down this obnoxious boy. The challenge that is Bryce Howell suddenly seems promising, making me feel more alive than I have in... well...forever.

Wendi L. Wilson

Chapter 2

School is finally over, and I'm walking home. Today was so strange. The rest of my classes went much the same as the first two. Bryce picked a different girl to sit by in each one, never picking me, thank God, and flirted shamelessly with each one. I tried to ignore him. On most counts, I failed. As much as I feel like I should dislike him, something draws me to him. I hate that it does.

I kick a pebble and watch it skid along the ground. The action pulls me out of my deep thoughts, and I become aware of footsteps behind me. I glance quickly over my shoulder and see him about ten yards back. I don't know how long he's been there, but I can only assume he has been since I left school. Emotion flares inside me. I don't know if it's anger, frustration or fear, but I feel the need to confront him.

I turn and glare, giving him a few seconds to reach me. He looks at me, curiosity making his eyes a shade lighter. I blow a few strands of my hair out of my face, tapping my foot until he stops in front of me.

"Why are you following me?" I demand, my voice angry.

He jerks back slightly at my words but recovers quickly, that sardonic smile fixed on his face. "What makes you think I'd ever follow you?"

I motion between us. "Uh, you're following me right now. It's creepy."

"Sorry to disappoint you, Kailani, but I'm just walking home."

"It's Kai," I say absentmindedly as I ponder his words. "You live this way?"

"Yeah."

"But, the only houses down this drive are mine and...oh."

"What?"

"You've moved into the old McCormick house, haven't you?"

"Is that the big white one down here next to the brick mansion?"

"Yeah. It is."

Suppressed

"Then, yes."

"I guess we're neighbors," I say.

I turn and start walking again. I mull over this news, remembering the moving van I saw heading onto the property just this morning. I feel stupid, not realizing that it must be Bryce's family as soon as I saw him. It would be too surreal if two different families moved to Santa Lorelei at the same time. I slow my steps, letting him catch up to me.

As he falls into step beside me, I say, "Sorry."

"Don't worry about it," he says. "You don't know me. It's easier for people like you to assume the worst."

"People like me?" I say, my hackles rising once more. "What do you mean people like me?"

"Santa Lorelei Island people," he says, as if he's discussing the weather and hadn't just insulted me. "Closed minded, stuck up, rich people."

We reach his driveway, and he turns off, walking away without another word as I bristle with indignation. I start to retort, scream at him that I am not closed minded, stuck up, or rich. That last bit cooled me like a bucket of ice water over my head. I start walking, picking up the pace until I'm in a near run.

Everyone at school knows I'm nothing more than a servant to Ms. Coraline. She makes a point to blab around town about her housemaid and her ungrateful brat of a daughter. That's why I don't have any friends other than Ana. She's the only one who would ever take a chance on me, getting to know me rather than judging me on my status as "the help."

I slow to a walk as I head onto Ms. Coraline's driveway. I realize Bryce is absolutely right in his assessment of the people on this island. They are closed minded and stuck up. They are definitely rich. I can't really fault him for lumping me in with the rest. Or maybe I can. He is being closed minded by assuming I'm rich and haughty. Screw him. I'm over it.

I want nothing more than to slam through the front door and bang it closed so hard Bryce will hear it all the way at the McCormick place, but I know better. Ms. Coraline is here somewhere, and I have to be careful or she'll put me to work. I close the door gently behind me, then tiptoe up the stairs to my room.

Suppressed

Once my bedroom door is closed behind me, I sigh a breath of relief. I pull open my backpack and sit on my bed, pulling out my homework. If I get it all done now, I'll have time for a swim later. I crack open my math book and start reading the problems, but the words blur and I can't concentrate.

The vision of catching Bryce checking out my butt in the office is playing on a loop in my head. I just don't get it. I would think it meant he liked what he saw, but his words and actions proved otherwise. He was distant and outright rude to me for most of the day.

I swipe my book off of my lap and stand, walking over to the mirror on the back of my closet door. I turn and, lifting up the back of my flannel, twist my head to see what I can of my backside. It's just as big and round as it always has been. I groan and walk back to my bed. Ana always tells me she'd kill for my butt because hers is as flat as an ironing board. I would switch with her in a heartbeat. Trying to find jeans that don't accentuate its gargantuan size is nearly impossible.

Thinking of Ana, I wonder why she wasn't at school. I would call her, but I don't have a cell phone. We can't afford it on mom's measly pay, and asking Ms. Coraline to use the house phone is out of the question. The one time I made that mistake, she laughed and told me phone privileges were not meant for the servants. God, I hate her. So much.

Knowing I won't find out about Ana until I see her, I decide to skip the rest of my homework and head out for a swim. I'm not getting anything done anyway. I can't concentrate, and I need to clear my head.

I undress and quickly slip on my favorite teal one piece. It has a thin skirt that helps to hide most of my butt. It makes me feel more secure even though I know no one will be down at the beach. There's no access, except from the houses, which is only ours and the McCormick place.

I pause just outside my door and huff. I guess I should start referring to it as the Howell place now. My heart starts to race. What if he's down there? Maybe I shouldn't go. It would ruin my swim if he were there, taunting me with that cryptic smile.

Steeling my spine, I close my door and walk quietly down the stairs. I refuse to let the thought of that boy ruin my one joy. If I allow the possibility of him showing up dictate my swims, I'd never go in the ocean again. That's unacceptable.

I grab a towel from the rack on the back porch, wrap it around my waist, and head down the wooden staircase that leads to the beach. A chilly breeze washes over me, bringing with it the scent of the sea and the sand. I breathe deeply, centering myself. This is my happy place- the one place where I can be myself. No pretenses.

I trudge through the sand, its cold temperature a balm to my bare feet. It's mid-November, so the water would probably be freezing to, well, everyone. The Pacific never gets very warm to start with, but by this time of year it's downright arctic. The cold doesn't affect me, though. I don't even notice the chill of the water as I drop my towel and wade out as fast as I can. As soon as I hit thigh-depth, I dive forward and swim out under the waves.

I cut through the water like a fish, swimming as far out as I can last before coming up for air. As my head breaks the surface, I tread water and look back toward the shore. I've made it farther than usual. Ms. Coraline's house looks like a doll house on a shelf from here. I smile. I love it when I beat my personal best.

I stretch out and start a slow breast stroke, letting my muscles lengthen and pull me through the water. After what I think is a mile, I turn in the water and head back in the other direction. I feel wonderful, the water chilling my skin as I dive under once more. When I come up for air again, I look and see that I'm back near the house. I flip and start a backstroke toward shore.

When the water is shallow enough, I stand and dunk my head backwards beneath the waves to slick my hair back. I turn and trudge toward shore, smiling at the freedom the ocean gives me. When I get close to the line where the waves are breaking, movement catches my eye. I look to the right where the old McCormick place stands tall and looming past a thicket of trees.

Standing on the back deck is a figure. I squint my eyes in the fading sun, but I can't make out any features. I get to the edge of the water and walk quickly toward my towel, reaching down to grab it and wrap it quickly around my torso. Shading my eyes with my hand, I look over at the neighbor's

Suppressed

deck once more. It's empty. Whoever was there, watching me, is now gone.

Wendi L. Wilson

Chapter 3

Dinner is a quiet affair. My mother and I eat at a small table in the kitchen after she serves Ms. Coraline in the main dining room. Mom is exhausted and not very talkative. She makes a half-hearted attempt to ask me about my day, but after a few noncommittal shrugs from me, she falls into silence. I help her clean the kitchen before heading up to my room.

I grab my books, plug earbuds into my ears, and sit on my bed to finish my homework. I finish quickly, the music keeping my mind free of distractions. I pack everything away, turn my music off and get ready for bed. Turning off the light, I slide beneath the covers, my muscles wonderfully tired from my swim.

My mind wanders back to the figure I saw watching me. I wonder if it was Bryce, then quickly shrug off the thought. He has no interest in me. There would be no reason for him to spy on me like that. Maybe it was one of his parents getting some air. Whoever it was probably didn't even see me. I drift off with these thoughts and have a deep, dreamless sleep.

I wake to my alarm, the blaring noise jerking me awake. I reach for the snooze button to stop the offensive sound. It's half past five, time to get up and start my chores. With a groan, I rise and head for the shower.

***

"Kailani! Where is the cream? I need cream for my tea!"

Ms. Coraline's voice grates on my nerves as she bellows from the parlor where she takes her morning tea. I flinch, silently berating myself for forgetting the cream. It's never a pleasure, serving her, but when I mess up, it's unbearable. She's a nasty old witch.

I walk quickly from the dining room where I was polishing the wooden table. My mom gives me a look as she hands me the cream. I take it and quickly walk from the room before she can start in on me. I don't know which is the worse of two evils, Ms. Coraline's reprimands or my mother's disappointed facial expression.

Suppressed

"I'm sorry, ma'am," I say, setting the cream on her tea service tray.

"Ungrateful chit," she sneers. "I take you in, let you live in my home, and this is what I get? An idiot who can't even remember simple instructions?"

"I'm sorry, ma'am," I repeat.

She dismisses me with a snarl, and I run quickly from the room. My mom meets me in the hall and tries to place a comforting hand on my shoulder. I jerk away and stalk back into the dining room. I scrub the table furiously, taking my frustration out on the already gleaming wood surface.

I can't understand why my mom makes us stay here. Ms. Coraline is horrible to both of us. She treats us like trash and yet, my mom stays, refusing to try to find another job in town. Anything, and I do mean anything, would be better than this. She's steadfast though, that this is where we need to be, and she won't explain why.

A hand puts pressure on mine, halting my furious motions. I glance up and meet my mother's green, sympathetic eyes. She pulls me up and wraps me in her arms, cocooning me in her warmth and love.

I feel like crying but resist the urge with a deep breath.

"You go on up and get ready for school. I'll finish here," she whispers.

All I can do is nod. I'm rendered mute by my efforts to hold back tears of frustration. I hustle from the room and up the stairs before Ms. Coraline decides to call me back for more berating. I close my bedroom door and mechanically prepare for school. I dress once more in jeans and a flannel, my standard wardrobe for this time of year.

I walk into the bathroom and pull my hair from its bandana, letting the flaming red lengths tumble down past my shoulders. I start to throw it up into a pony tail but change my mind at the last minute. Running a wide toothed comb through it, I part it on the side and swoop the front over my forehead. The loose waves frame my face as I apply some lip gloss and pinch my cheeks.

I stop and stare into my own eyes, wondering why I'm suddenly trying a little harder with my appearance. I've never cared before. My blue eyes narrow as I decide to stop fooling myself. I know why I'm doing it. It's because of *him*.

Suppressed

Disgusted with myself but leaving my hair as it is, I turn off the light and head downstairs with my backpack slung over one shoulder. It's a little early, but I decide to leave anyway. Maybe I won't see him if I leave now. I can get to school and slip into my seat in the back of homeroom, all without having to endure that smirk on his stupid, handsome face.

I reach the end of our drive and turn right, staring at the ground in front of me. As I pass the driveway of the Old McCormick, uh, Howell place, a set of hiking boots appears next to mine, falling into step beside me.

Startled, I look up at Bryce's face, but he's staring straight ahead, not looking at me. I decide two can play at that game and face forward without speaking. I try speeding up, but he stays on pace with me without even looking like he's putting in any effort. I slow down, he slows down.

"Ugh, what do you want?"

"Good morning to you, too, Kai."

I can't bring myself to regret my snappish tone. This guy was downright rude to me all day yesterday and now, suddenly, he wants to be friendly? I don't get it, and his mood swings are giving me whiplash. I grunt in response and refuse to comment. We walk in silence until we reach the school parking lot.

"See you later," he says, speeding his steps until he's well ahead of me.

I slowly shuffle my feet as I watch his retreating back. I can't believe it. He's made it pretty obvious that he doesn't want to be seen with me. He heads straight for a cluster of kids near the entrance of the building, smiling and waving hello. Laughter erupts as I near. I glance up and see several girls shooting me sly looks. Apparently, I am the butt of some joke they've made.

I push past them and stalk to class, fuming. I don't know what's the matter with me. The nasty remarks and gossip have never bothered me before. I hate all these people, so why would I care? Suddenly, this new guy shows up, and I get offended. I'm ashamed of myself.

My mood brightens as Ana walks through the door and makes a beeline for the seat beside me. Her long black hair gleams under the florescent lights as she plops into the desk beside me with a sigh. Her black kohl eyeliner looks smeared, and her nose has a reddish tinge, standing out from the light brown skin of her face.

"You okay?" I whisper.

"Yeah," she says, sighing again. "I was sick all weekend, but my fever broke last night and Mama said I had to come back to school today. I still feel like crap, though."

"Well, I'm glad you're here."

Ana smiles. "What did I miss? You look pissed."

The sound of many feet captures our attention, and we both glance toward the front of the room. A gaggle of girls walks in, giggling like a bunch of morons. Directly behind them, *he* walks in. I look at Ana, whose face lights up as her mouth forms a silent "O." She slides her eyes to me, silently asking the question.

"New kid," I whisper. "He's a jerk."

Ana's eyebrows shoot up, and I know why. I groan inwardly. I never notice anyone enough to have a strong reaction to them. I go with the flow, letting insults and innuendoes fly over my head. She can tell this guy has gotten under my skin. I blush and look down at my desk, pulling out my notebook as

Mr. Jonas clears his throat to bring silence to the room.

She pulls out a piece of scrap paper and writes furiously for a few seconds. Folding the paper into quarters, she flicks it in my direction, landing it on my desk with unerring accuracy. I quickly cup my hand over it, hiding it from view as Mr. Jonas glances around the room. Once he looks back at his role book, I pull the note into my lap and open it.

Lunch outside. I need the scoop.

I glance at her and nod quickly, crumpling the paper into a ball and shoving it into the pocket of my jeans. Class drags on as we are instructed to pull out our math books and complete the exercises on page eighty-five.

I'm distracted again, unable to concentrate as I sneak several glances at Bryce. He's sitting beside Lanie Thompson today. He's making his way through the entire female population of the junior class and, for some reason, it pisses me off. He really is a jerk.

As I watch, his shoulders twitch and he rolls them. Before I can look away, he glances over his shoulder and catches my eye. Before I can react, his eyes are back on Lanie's book, and I'm still staring at the back of his head. A flash of heat sears my body. He caught me staring. Again.

Ana doesn't bring up the subject of Bryce until we're sitting at a picnic table under the large oak tree behind the school. I am picking at my chili mac, trying to decide if it's actually edible when she slides onto the bench next to me and pushes my tray away. She hands me a sandwich from her lunch sack and pulls one out for herself.

"Thanks."

She waves it off. "Forget about it. Now, spill."

I groan, but she waves that off too. "There's not much to tell," I say, feeling my cheeks heat with the lie.

"You're lying," she says, her face brightening. Her face breaks into a self-satisfied smile. "I knew it. You like him!"

"Shh. Not so loud," I whisper, glancing around to see if anyone overheard.

"No one heard me, Chica. It's just us. Tell me everything."

I take a deep breath and lean in close. I tell her everything, even the fact that I caught him staring at my butt. When I'm finished, she leans back, her lips pressed tight and her brow furrowed. She absentmindedly takes a bite of her sandwich, chewing slowly as I start to fidget.

"Well?" I ask, finally losing patience.

"It sounds like he's trying to make you jealous."

"That's absurd."

"Boys are absurd," she shoots back. "He was checking you out, so he must've liked what he saw. If I know you, and I do, you probably did a good job of ignoring him and pretending like you weren't interested. Wait," she says, holding up a hand as I start to interrupt at that bit about pretending, "You can play it off with him but not me. You're interested." She pauses for effect, and when I hold my silence, she continues. "So, he thinks you're playing hard to get."

"I don't know, Ana. That seems a little farfetched to me."

"Why?"

"I mean..." I pause, trying to think of the right words. "You've seen him! He could have any girl at this school. I'm pretty sure most of them have already made an offer. Why on earth would he want me?"

Ana grunted. "Have you looked in the mirror lately?"

I shake my head at her. Of course, I've looked in the mirror. I'm a red-headed, freckle-faced freak. I don't have the expensive clothes or jewelry that the rest of the girls here have. I have a huge rear end, and not in a good way, despite what Ana tries to tell me. My figure is definitely not what you'd call "hourglass." I'm not overweight, but other than the round curve of my butt, I have the straight lines of a boy.

"I have, and I know what he sees when he looks at me. A ginger with small boobs and a big butt."

Ana frowns at me. "I really wish you'd stop calling yourself that! Even if I agreed with that term- which I don't- you don't even fit the bill. Your hair is a gorgeous shade of deep red that women all over the world pay good money to achieve and that tiny grouping of freckles across your nose is adorable."

"Okay, okay. I give up. I'll stop calling myself a ginger but I still refuse to believe that Bryce Howell wants me."

"But you admit that you do want him?"

"Hey now, I never said that!"

"But you didn't deny it either."

I give her a pained look but hold my silence. Honestly, I don't know what I think about him. He's very handsome. There's no denying that. He's also arrogant and at most times outright rude. He makes me angry almost every time I see him, but I am intrigued. I'd love to crack his shell and see what's really inside.

"Hello."

Ana and I both jerk our heads up at the word. As if I'd conjured him, Bryce is standing next to the table with a tray of food in his hands. He gestures with it, silently asking if he can sit. I nod at the same time as Ana, and Bryce slides onto the bench across from us.

"Hi, I'm Ana Fuentes," she says, holding out a hand for him to shake. She nods in my direction. "This one's best friend."

Suppressed

"Bryce," he says, taking her hand and pumping it once before releasing it. "But I'm sure Kai has told you all about me."

I suck in a breath which carries a piece of food into my windpipe. I cough harshly, trying to hack it out so I can breathe. Ana pats my back as my eyes start watering. When the coughing subsides, I take a long gulp of water. I can feel my face burning with embarrassment. Again.

"You okay?" he asks me.

I look at him to see he is barely repressing a smile. "Fine, thanks." I clear my throat again.

"Where did you move from?" Ana asks, changing the subject and saving me from further embarrassment.

"Southern California," he says around a mouth full of chili mac.

"So not too far then, eh?"

"No. My dad still works in Los Angeles, so he takes the ferry to the mainland and back every day."

"That's cool," Ana says.

"What does he do?" I ask, determined to get into the conversation.

"He's a lawyer at a big firm in the city."

I nod, unable to think of anything else to say. His dad is a big shot attorney; my mom is a house maid. We have *so* much in common. I make a scoffing noise, and it draws Bryce's attention. He raises his eyebrows at me before his eyes dart away.

Ana asks a few more questions, keeping the conversation going. I silently listen but keep my mouth closed. I obviously can't control my feelings around Bryce and nothing slips past his notice. It's like he's tuned in to my every emotion. I don't like it.

I must be frowning because he gives me that highbrow look again. I shake my head and smile brightly, hoping it doesn't look too fake. Then, I make the mistake of looking into his eyes. I stare as his eyebrows lower a centimeter at a time until they are drawn low over his eyes, giving them a hooded look.

He stands, his movements abrupt. "It was nice to meet you, Ana. Bye." He nods at her and without looking back at me, he stalks away.

"Well, that was weird."

Suppressed

"I told you he doesn't like me."

Ana stared thoughtfully at his retreating back. "I wouldn't be so sure."

Wendi L. Wilson

Chapter 4

I skip down the steps to the beach and take off in a dead run as soon as my feet hit the sand. Throwing my towel to the ground as I near the water, I slosh into the foamy waves and dive headfirst without stopping. I swim out even farther than yesterday, needing space only the sea can give me.

I have been nothing but a mass of pent up energy since lunch. My conversation with Ana about Bryce and our stilted lunch encounter with him have had me tied in knots all day. I'm nervous and confused. I don't know whether or not to believe Ana, that Bryce might like me, or if I even want him to.

I dive under, keeping my eyes open, and head toward the ocean floor. There aren't many fish around, but I do spot a blue crab scuttling along the sand. I turn and head back to the surface. I doggy paddle around for a while, enjoying the feeling of the crisp water against my hot skin. When I feel the muscles in my arms starting to strain, I head back toward shore.

I stumble tiredly from the water and fall backwards onto the soft, cold sand. I check the watch on my wrist, which is, thankfully, waterproof, and see that I was out in the water for over an hour. The cool evening air kisses my skin as the sun starts to set so I pull myself up and look around, searching for my towel.

"Here you go."

I shriek in surprise and spin around to see Bryce standing a few feet away holding my towel. I stare at him with wide eyes for a few seconds, trying to figure out where he had come from. I didn't see him when I trudged from the water. I'm sure he wasn't there.

He shakes the towel, urging me to take it from him. I step forward and snatch it from his hand, wrapping it quickly around my torso. I don't speak until I'm sure everything is covered. I look at him and frown, making my displeasure obvious.

"Where did you come from? Are you spying on me?"

He shoots me that smile I hate so much and says, "I came from there," he points to his house, "and no. I was not spying, per se."

"Per se?"

"Well, to be completely honest, I was sitting on my deck when you went out. I watched you swimming, then came down here when you came out of the water. I only just got here."

"You were watching me?" My voice is softer now.

He nods. "Well, I saw you streaking toward the water like your life depended on it. I thought something was wrong, and I was going to go after you but..."

"But?" Somehow my traitorous feet bring me closer to him.

"You dove into the water and shot out like a rocket. It was amazing how far you got, so fast. Where'd you learn to swim like that?"

I smile. Swimming, I can talk about. "I don't know. It's always been that way for me, I guess. I grew up swimming here, and I go out every day if I can. It's my happy place."

"Isn't it cold?"

My smile grows bigger as I nod. "The water is freezing, but I don't know." I shrug, my mouth still stretched wide. "It doesn't bother me. I'm just used to it, I guess. I've been doing this all my life."

My joy must be infectious, because his mouth lifts into a wide smile. I almost choke again when I see it. This smile...it's a real one. The first I've seen on him. My belly churns, and I silently thank God it's dusk because I'm sure my face is bright red again. I swallow thickly and look down at my feet.

"Okay, well, I guess I'll see you tomorrow then?"

I take this as a dismissal and nod before quickly turning and shuffling through the sand toward the staircase that leads up to Ms. Coraline's house. I hear what sounds like a sigh behind me. The sound probably came from the surf, so I keep moving forward.

I pick my way up the wooden steps, and when I reach the top I turn my head and peek over my shoulder. He's still in the same spot. I can't see his expression in the darkening light, but I can tell he's watching me. I jerk my head back and blush at being caught, but I can't suppress the smile that comes.

My thoughts of Bryce carry me into the house, the smile still plastered on my face, making me clumsy. As soon as I close the door behind me, I realize my mistake. I hear the tap, tap, tap of a shoe and turn quickly to see Ms. Coraline standing there, a nasty frown marring her face.

Suppressed

"Go to the kitchen, and get the pot of tea from your mother. Bring it to my parlor, now. There are some things you and I need to discuss."

I nod mutely, knowing that any comment, regardless of what it is, will be interpreted as back-talk and whatever she has in store for me will be ten times worse. I wish I could ask to go change out of my wet bathing suit, but I know better. I rush to the kitchen, gripping the edges of my towel around my waist.

"Tea," I say urgently to my mother, who's already pouring boiling water into the porcelain teapot.

"What did you do?"

I frown at my mom. "What makes you think I did anything?"

"She's making you bring her tea. Kailani, just tell me."

"I don't know," I grit out through clenched teeth. "I just went for a swim, and she caught me coming back into the house. I didn't do anything. I swear, Mom."

"Just go," she says, pushing the tea service tray into my hands. "Come see me when she's done talking to you."

I walk as quickly as I can without dropping the tray, knowing that things will only be worse for me if Ms. Coraline feels like she's been kept waiting. The parlor doors are open, so I step through and head straight for the coffee table to set the tray down. I stand back as Ms. Coraline leaves her station by the window, walking past me to sit in one of the chairs.

"I see you remembered the cream this time," she says, the disdain obvious in her voice.

I keep my silence, biting back the scathing remark on the tip of my tongue. I watch as her pudgy fingers spoon sugar and pour cream into her tea. My eyes travel over her. It looks like she's put on a few extra pounds recently. Her chunky butt barely fits in the chair. One side of my mouth lifts at the thought.

"And just what is so funny?"

My mouth drops immediately, and my gaze falls to the floor. I curse myself internally for the mistake. "Nothing, ma'am," I mumble.

She grunts but decides to let the issue of my impertinence pass...at least for the moment. "I want to talk to you about what I saw through this very window a little while ago."

My eyes shoot back to her face, confusion screwing up my eyebrows. "What you saw, ma'am? I only went for a swim."

"Don't lie to me, girl. I saw you talking to that Howell boy down on the beach."

I shake my head, wondering how she even knows who he is. "I-"

"Save your excuses. I know what I saw. You are, from this point on, to avoid that boy at all costs. Don't speak to him. Don't even look at him. Do you understand me?"

"But..." I trail off, seeing the look of impending rage crossing her face. I know not to question her. "Yes, ma'am."

"Good. Now get out of here and change before you drip any more water on my carpet."

I rush from the room and run up the stairs. I know my mother is waiting for me in the kitchen, but I have to get to my sanctuary. Besides, the old hag ordered me to change. I dart into my bedroom and close the door gently behind me.

"Don't look at him?" I ask the room. "What on earth?"

Shaking my head, I strip out of my bathing suit and bundle up in my robe. I gather some clothes and crack open my door. Peeking out, I look first right, then left. The hall is empty, so I dash across to the bathroom.

After showering and dressing, I head back to my room. My mom is sitting on the bed, waiting for me. She motions for me to close the door. I push it closed and turn back to my mother. She waves me toward her, the motion quick and erratic.

"What did Ms. Coraline say?"

I shrug, confusion crossing my face. "She said she saw me talking to the neighbor after my swim. You know, the new boy next door? She forbade me from ever talking to him again. Can you believe that?"

Mom's face tightens. "Well, make sure you don't."

"What? Mom! This is ridiculous!"

"Shh. Lower your voice."

Suppressed

I lean in close and whisper harshly. "She. Is. Your. Boss. She can order us around in this house, but she can't tell me who I can and can't be friends with. Why are you taking her side?"

Mom's face doesn't even twitch. "We live here, and you know we can't leave. Please, Kai, just follow her rules, okay?"

My anger rises even higher. "Why can't we leave?" I demand. "You can find a new job, mom. We could move, and we wouldn't have to deal with her shi...crap ever again."

Just as she does every time I suggest this, mom shakes her head, a sad expression etched across her features. "I'm sorry, Baby, but we can't."

Without further explanation, my mom rises and kisses the top of my head. She walks, her steps slow and measured, to the door. Pulling it open, she pauses and turns back before leaving. She gives me another sad smile and says, "Please, Kailani. Don't cross her. We can't afford it," then walks out, closing the door gently behind her.

I lay across my bed with a groan. I tell myself I'm more upset about the old witch ordering me around, not about the actual order. She has no right to tell me who I can or can't talk to. I roll over and scream into my pillow to muffle the sound. I pound my fist into it a few times for good measure.

"I don't even like him," I whisper. "He's a jerk with a superiority complex."

Once I have myself convinced that never talking to him again is actually a blessing, I roll out of bed and set about drying my hair. I take special care to dry it slowly while pulling a brush through it, making the red strands perfectly straight and crackling with fire. I tie a large bandana around it in the hopes that it will protect my hard work, keeping it from turning into a tangled rat's nest while I sleep.

I dress in sweats and a t-shirt, then head down to the kitchen, hoping my mother kept a plate warm for me. As I pass the parlor, I hear my mother's voice, the palpable deference almost making me lose my appetite. I stop just beside the doors, which are pulled closed but not quite touching. A small crack between them allows the sound to travel out into the hall.

"Well, she better take heed," Ms. Coraline says with finality. "If I see her talking to that...boy again, I will follow through. Don't doubt it, Merryn."

"She won't, ma'am. I talked to her. She assured me that she will obey you."

"I certainly hope you're right. I'd hate for her to have to face the consequences."

I skip away, hearing my mother's light footsteps heading toward the doors. I run to the kitchen, where I try to regain my breath before my mom appears. I wonder what Ms. Coraline meant by consequences. She said she'd hate for me to face them, but her voice sounded positively gleeful. I can't help but scowl.

"Oh, hey Kai."

Mom's voice startles me from my brooding thoughts. I wipe my face clear of emotion before turning to face her. "Hey, mom. Can I get some food?"

"Of course, baby," she says, bending to pull a plate from the oven.

I take the plate and set it on the counter, opting to stand while I eat. I watch my mother as she putters around the kitchen, silently willing her to bring up her conversation with Ms. Coraline. I want to know what the old hag meant but not enough to out myself for eavesdropping. I've been in trouble too many times for that already.

"Wash your plate when you're done, okay?"

I nod as she finally meets my eyes. I see a quick flash of worry in hers before she blinks it away. She kisses my forehead and leaves the room, taking my appetite with her. I scrape the leftover food into the trash, scrub my plate and fork in the sink, and grab a bottle of water from the fridge before turning off the light and heading back up to my room.

Chapter 5

I watch my feet as I walk up the road. I've been kicking the same rock for the last dozen yards, trying to keep my mind off Bryce and the fact that his driveway is getting closer and closer with each step I take. Why is it that I've never wanted to see him quite as badly as I do this morning, after I've been warned to never even look at him again?

I know the answer to that. It's Ms. Coraline, and that she's the one doing the ordering. I hate her. And not the classic teenager version of hate where everything is blown out of proportion. This is real, true hate. I do the opposite of what she wants as often as possible. As long as I won't get caught, I savor the rebellious victories whenever I can.

I haven't always hated her. She's always been haughty and stand-offish, but as a child, I just assumed this was a normal way for adults to behave. It wasn't until I was seven that her true evil nature made itself known to me. That day has been etched into my brain forever. I'll never forget. I'll never forgive. Never.

Wendi L. Wilson

It was a sunny summer day, and mom and I had spent the afternoon in town. Mom bought me an ice cream cone, and as we walked home, the vanilla goodness started melting and dripping down my hand. I stopped to wipe my hand on my shirt while mom walked ahead. I heard a sound coming from the bushes and, forgetting the sticky mess on my hands and face, crept closer to investigate.

I caught sight of a tiny pair of eyes before a high-pitched mewling sound met my ears. I dropped to my knees and coaxed the small, black kitten forward. I picked her up, smoothing her jet-black fur and whispering in soothing tones. As I cuddled her, she licked the smeared ice cream from my face. Laughing, I held my cone up, letting her sniff it before she started licking it in earnest.

Hearing my mom's voice calling me from the driveway, I shoved the kitten beneath my shirt and ran all the way to the house, passing mom quickly before she could figure out what I was up to. I ran toward the front door, imagining where I could hide her in my room and how I was going to sneak milk and food to feed her.

Suppressed

As my free hand reached for the doorknob, it turned and the door swung open, revealing Ms. Coraline. I took a quick step back, lowering my head in greeting as my mother had taught me. I waited with eyes downcast for her to move aside so I could pass, praying the kitten would keep quiet.

I was naive. Of course, the old witch's eagle eyes had spotted the lump under my shirt. She cleared her throat, bringing my gaze up to her narrowed eyes. I held my breath, a silent litany rolling on repeat through my head. Please let me keep her. Please let me keep her.

"Well, what do we have here?"

Her voice sounded pleasant, so I pulled the furry, black bundle from beneath my shirt and held it up for her inspection. I smiled proudly, as Ms. Coraline took the struggling kitten from my chubby hand.

I heard my mother's footsteps coming to a halt behind me, followed by a short gasp. I turned to smile at her, but the grin dropped from my face when I saw her expression. I didn't understand it at the time, but I know now what it was. Horror.

I turned back to Ms. Coraline. "May I please keep her, ma'am?" I asked, using my most polite voice, as my mother had taught me.

"May you keep her?" she asked, her pleasant expression dropping from her face in an instant. "May you keep her, you ask?"

"Ma'am," my mother started.

"No, Merryn. This is between me and this child." She grabbed the scruff of the kitten's neck and let its body dangle, then shook it violently, looking back at me. "You want to bring this," she said, shaking the kitten roughly again, "dirty fleabag into my house?"

"Please, ma'am, you're hurting her."

I'll never forget her smile. It was pure evil, her eyes narrow and lipstick staining her teeth. I shivered, not really understanding what was happening. It didn't take long for me to figure it out.

Holding the kitten aloft, she grabbed the fleshy part of my upper arm and jerked me forward. I watched my ice cream drop to the wooden floor of the porch as she dragged me into the house. I fought her grip at first, but she only dug her long nails harder into my skin, making me quit my struggling and walk faster to keep up. We walked quickly through the house to the back door, my mother following silently behind.

She dragged me through the back door, all the way down the wooden staircase to the beach. We trudged quickly through the sand, my eyes burning as I tried to fight back the tears. I was scared and my arm hurt and I didn't know what we were doing down by the water. She released my arm and held the kitten up in front of my face.

"You need to learn a lesson," she said, her voice strong and determined.

"Yes, ma'am," I said, not really sure what she expected me to say.

"I will not tolerate any animals in my house," she said shooting a meaningful look behind me at my mother. Glancing back at me, she smiled that evil smile again. "You are to blame for this."

I scrunched my eyes in confusion, not understanding what she meant. Before I had a chance to question her, she pulled back her arm then slung it forward, a high-pitched screech ringing in my ears as I watched the small kitten fly through the air and land with a splash in the sea.

My breath whooshed out of my chest on a scream as I took a step into the foamy water. I had every intention of swimming out to save the poor creature, but Ms. Coraline's sharp talons once again gripped my arm, keeping me where I was.

"Hey."

I jerk to a stop, that one soft word pulling me from the memory. Bryce stops as well, looking at me through squinted eyes. He cocks his head to the side, studying me.

"You okay?" he asks. "You looked like you were a million miles away."

"Fine," I say, shooting a quick look over my shoulder.

He looks in that direction, too, then back at me. "Are you sure? You seem kind of jumpy."

"I said I'm fine," I snap as I start walking again.

I hasten my footsteps, hoping he'll get the hint let me be. As much as I wanted to see him before, the memory of Ms. Coraline's vindictiveness has changed my mind. I can't chance talking to him.

Suppressed

There's no telling what the old woman will do if she finds out.

My hopes are dashed as I hear his footsteps shuffle quickly to catch up. I see him in my periphery but decide not to acknowledge him. Maybe if I ignore him, he'll give up. My nerves are wound up, waiting to see what he'll do.

"Did I do something to piss you off?" he asks when we've walked about a quarter mile in silence.

I suck in a deep breath and sigh. I stop walking and look behind me once more. No one but me and Bryce are on the road, and we're far enough away from the house that Ms. Coraline couldn't possibly see us. I motion for Bryce to follow as I step to the side of the road and skirt the large bushes planted there. I keep walking, not looking back to see if he followed, until I am buried deep in a copse of trees out of sight of the road and any cars that may pass.

When I've gone far enough, I stop and turn around. A large body crashes into mine and arms circle around me, stopping me from tumbling to the side as I instinctively try to jump back. My body flashes cold then hot, frozen in his warm embrace. I'm not sure if I should try to extricate myself from his grip or pull him in closer and snuggle against his chest. I seriously consider the latter before he takes the decision from me, releasing me and taking a small step back.

"Sorry," he says, rubbing a hand across the back of his neck. "I thought you were going to fall."

The action causes the white thermal to strain against his muscled chest, which I'm still staring at in a daze. Reality crashes in, and I lift my gaze to his, wiping the back of my hand against my mouth to make sure there's no drool. One dark brow shoots up, and I know I'm busted. He caught me checking him out...again. I clear my throat, closing my eyes for a moment to regain control of myself.

"Thanks," I whisper, opening my eyes to stare into his once more.

I see a smile flash across his face before it drops as he looks from me to our surroundings. "What's with all the cloak and dagger stuff? Are you ashamed to be seen talking to me?"

One side of my mouth lifts into a lopsided grin. "Yeah, right," I say under my breath before I raise my voice to a normal level. "Of course not. It's...complicated."

I watch his arms cross his chest as he says, "Try me."

I glance upward at the patches of blue sky I can see through the canopy of bare tree limbs. I don't know how to explain. I don't even know why I feel the need to explain this to him at all, but I do. The idea of him thinking I'm ashamed to be seen with him turns my stomach. I look back at him and sigh.

"I've been forbidden to speak to you."

His head jerks back as if I had slapped him as a look of disbelief crosses his face. "Excuse me?"

I shake my head. "You heard me, Bryce. I'm not allowed to see you, talk to you...anything. It has been decreed," I say with a hint of sarcasm.

"Why would your mom..."

He trails off as I shake my head again. "Not my mom. Ms. Coraline, herself, has ordered me to stay away from you. She saw us talking last night on the beach and lost it."

"But, why?"

"I have no idea."

"Wait," he says, shaking his head and pacing back and forth in front of me. "Isn't the old lady your mom's boss?" At my nod, he continues, "Does she really think she can tell you what to do? I mean, you're not her kid. What did your mom say?"

I put my hand out and grasp his forearm, stopping his agitated pacing. "I have to do what she says. I don't really know what will happen, but if my mom's reaction is any indication, it's bad."

His eyes are glued to my hand. I jerk it away from him, my face heating with a blush. Bryce lifts his blue gaze to meet mine, and I feel like a rabbit in a snare. I can't move. Can't breathe. Bumble bees erupt in my belly. My heart starts to flutter in time with their angry buzzing. I swallow thickly, forcing myself to hold his stare.

"So," he says in a low voice, taking a step closer, "if you're not allowed to see me, why are we here?"

I refuse to back up, even though he's so close I can feel the heat emanating from his body. Keeping eye contact, I say, "Because I refuse to let that old hag tell me what to do."

Suppressed

His smile reinvigorates the buzzing in my belly. "Is that the only reason?" he asks, his voice almost a whisper as he leans in even closer.

I suck in a broken breath, forcing my eyes to stay open and focused on his. "No." No? Why did I say no? Yes! I meant yes! Oh, God.

He flashes me one of those real smiles, the one I saw last night on the beach, and takes a step back. "Good to know," he says before turning and strolling away.

I close my eyes and grind my teeth together, concentrating on taking slow breaths. When I open them, he's gone. Disappointment races through my body. I don't know what I hoped for, but this isn't it. He left without even saying "bye" or "see ya later" or anything.

"Good to know," I mumble. "What does that even mean?"

I head back out onto the road and look both ways, but Bryce is nowhere to be seen. Turning right, I start the slow walk to school. I'm so deep in thought, trying to figure out the enigma of Bryce, that a shock zips through me when I suddenly find myself in the school parking lot. Shaking my head to clear it, I pick up my pace and head for the doors.

"Kai!"

I turn my head toward the sound of my name and see Ana running toward me. I stop, waiting for her to catch up. When she reaches my side, we turn as one and head for the entrance of the school.

"What's up, Chica?" she asks.

"Nothing."

She grabs my arm and pulls me to a halt. Her brown eyes lock onto mine for a few seconds before she wraps her hand around my elbow and pulls me to the left, away from the school doors and around the corner to the back. When we are far enough away not to be heard by the arriving students, she releases me and taps her foot.

"What?" I ask, cringing at the defensive tremor I hear in my voice.

"That's a good question," she says, tapping a finger against her lips. "What is it? What's happened?"

I shake my head and try to wipe away the frown I feel pulling my lips down. "It's nothing, really."

Suppressed

"Kailani."

I groan, knowing that tone. She won't let up until I tell her. I let my shoulders droop and lean my body against the wall. Shrugging my backpack off my shoulder, it drops to the ground with a thud.

"It's Bryce."

Her eyes widen, then narrow, sparkling with humor. "I knew it!"

"Keep your voice down," I urge, looking over her shoulder to see if anyone heard her and thought to investigate.

"Sorry, Kai. What's happened now?" she asks in a quiet voice.

"Last night he came to the beach while I was swimming. We only talked for a few minutes, but when I got back to the house, Ms. Coraline summoned me to her parlor."

"Uh oh."

"Right?" I shake my head with a sigh. "She forbade me to see him. Said I couldn't speak to him or even look at him."

"What? She has no right..."

"Apparently, she does," I cut in. "I talked to my mom, and she said I have to obey her."

Ana frowns and shakes her head. I thought it was ridiculous when my mom told me to do as Ms. Coraline says, and it's comforting that Ana agrees with me. It makes me remember how glad I am to have her as my best friend. She's always on my side, no matter what.

"So, is that all?"

"Isn't that enough?"

A grin flashes across her face as she says, "That's nothing. You and I both know you'll go out of your way to see him if for no other reason than to cross the old witch." When I only smile, she continues, "So what else happened?"

My face falls. "I saw him this morning."

"And?"

"And I told him what happened. I pulled him into the woods where we wouldn't be seen and told him everything the old hag said."

"What did he say?"

"He seemed really agitated at first, like he was upset that I'd been ordered to stay away from him. Then he asked me why I was with him, why I pulled him into the woods to tell him, if I wasn't allowed to speak to him."

"What did you say?"

"I told him I don't let Ms. Coraline tell me what to do."

"Kai, you're blushing! What are you not telling me?"

I take a deep breath to try and quell the bees that erupt in my belly. "He asked me if that was the only reason I was there...and I said no."

Ana's head jerks back in surprise. With a brilliant smile, she asks, "What did he say?"

"Good to know."

"Good to know? What does that mean?"

I shake my head. "I don't know. He disappeared before I could ask him."

"What do you mean disappeared?"

I shrug my shoulders. "I don't know. When I opened my eyes, he'd disappeared."

"Why were your eyes closed?"

I flinch. I hadn't meant to reveal that bit of information. "Well...okay, God, Ana, I'll tell you. I was embarrassed. As we talked he kept coming closer and closer. By the time he asked if that was the only reason I was there, I'd lost my senses entirely. He was so close, I thought he was going to kiss me or something."

"Did you want him to? No, don't answer that. Of course, you did."

Refusing to confirm or deny her statement, I continue. "Then he backs up suddenly, says 'good to know' and walks away. I closed my eyes to regain my composure, and when I opened them, he was gone."

Ana stares at me, but her eyes are unfocused, and I can tell she's thinking. She nods as if coming to a conclusion and refocuses on me. Threading her arm through mine, she nods toward my backpack. I pick it up, and we head back toward the front of the building.

"Aren't you going to say anything?" I ask when the silence becomes intolerable.

Ana leans in so that her mouth is close to my ear. "He likes you," she whispers.

Suppressed

"I don't..." I start to say, but she shakes her head as we come around the corner and wind our way through a group of students heading for the doors.

"Later," she says.

I nod in agreement. All sorts of arguments against her conclusion wind their way through my mind as we part ways and head to our lockers. Bryce Howell can have any single girl at this school, maybe even the taken ones, with the exception of Ana. Why would he want an awkward, freckle-faced redhead with a creepy old lady hell-bent on keeping her away from him? He wouldn't.

But I can't deny the feeling that rushed through my body when Ana whispered those three words. For just a moment, I believed her, and the feeling was amazing. Elation. That's the best word I can come up with to describe it. I was elated.

I shake myself, pulling my head out of the clouds and back down to earth. If Bryce does like me, he has a funny way of showing it. Of course, what would I know about boys and how they show their feelings? Nothing, I admit to myself. Not a single thing. I close my locker and walk slowly toward Mr. Jonas's class.

Wendi L. Wilson

Chapter 6

I walk into homeroom and see Ana waving to me from the back, an empty desk beside her. I put my head down and make my way down the aisle. Plopping into my seat, I look at her, hoping to continue our conversation before Mr. Jonas arrives and starts calling the roll.

I lean toward her to speak, but one look at her has me straightening in my chair. Her face is glowing as she leans forward and smiles at someone on my other side. I whip my head to the left and suck in a harsh breath.

"Bryce."

The word comes out as a choked whisper. He was staring intently at the front of the class, but at the sound of his name, he turns his head and shoots me a roguish grin. Once again, those darn bees take up residence in my stomach.

"Yes, Kailani?"

I jerk my eyes toward the front as Mr. Jonas closes the classroom door and heads toward his desk. He opens his laptop and calls names out in a monotone voice. I squeak out a "here" when he calls my name and hear Ana giggle. I shoot her a death stare, and she sobers quickly.

"Okay, class, pull out your math books and turn to page eighty-eight."

As I flip the pages of my book, I feel a tap on my left shoulder. I glance over, turning my head as little as possible. Bryce is leaning toward me, motioning with his hands. I swivel my head in his direction, and he smiles. Pointing at the open book on my desk, he mouths, "Can we share?"

The bees work themselves into a frenzy as I nod and push the book slightly in his direction. A loud screech echoes throughout the room as he scoots his desk toward me while still sitting in it. Every head in the room jerks toward us, and I feel my face heat up. Before I drop my gaze to my lap, I see several sets of narrowed eyes shooting daggers at me. The junior girls are not happy with this development.

"Mr. Howell, I thought I gave you a textbook yesterday."

"Sorry, Mr. Jonas. I left it at home. It won't happen again."

Suppressed

I peek up through my eyelashes at our teacher to gauge his reaction. He looks dazed for a moment before shaking it off and turning his back to the class to write on the board. I turn incredulous eyes toward Bryce, who is leaning in close and staring intently at my math book. I've never known Mr. Jonas to let an unprepared student go without a lecture. I look over at Ana, whose head is swiveling back and forth between Mr. Jonas and Bryce with raised eyebrows. She meets my gaze, and I shrug, mouthing, "Weird, right?" before refocusing on Mr. Jonas and attempting to take notes.

My determination to be a model student is short-lived. Bryce scoots his desk a fraction closer, leaning in and snaking his arm behind me, resting it on the back of my chair. My breath hitches in my throat. I silently curse myself, and him, when the corner of his mouth lifts slightly. He's enjoying this.

I redouble my efforts to pay attention to the lecture. Bryce is playing with me, relishing my obvious discomfort. I steel my spine and ignore his proximity. I know I can do this. Pretend he's not here. Pretend I can't feel the warmth of his body against my side and smell the fresh scent of citrusy soap in my nostrils. I feel nothing. That's my new mantra.

It seems to be working until I feel a light brush against the side of my arm. I look down and see Bryce's hand resting on the back of my chair, his thumb sweeping light strokes against my arm. I raise my head and take a deep, calming breath before turning to him with a raised brow. I'm determined to play this cool.

He's staring at his notebook, scribbling out math problems. There's no cocky grin, no look of innocence, nothing. As I watch, his eyebrows screw up in concentration, trying to work out a difficult step in the math problem. All the while, his thumb continues to lightly caress my arm. He doesn't even realize he's doing it and for some reason that makes me smile.

He glances up and catches me with the grin on my face. Smiling back, he whispers, "What's so funny?"

Shaking my head, I refocus my gaze on my own notebook and try to will away the blush I feel heating my face. I know he can see it. My embarrassment ratchets up a notch as I think

Suppressed

about how I must look. With my red hair and freckles, my blushes are never flattering.

My heart skips a beat, then pounds double time as Bryce wraps his whole hand around my bicep and softly strokes it. Up and down. Up and down. Each pass causes my breath to hitch as I try desperately to ignore it. Before I realize he's moved, I feel his breath on my neck.

"I love it when you blush," he whispers near my ear.

My brain searches for words, a comeback, something coy or charming, but my mind won't work. Before I can think of anything, Bryce straightens, pulling his arm from around me. I let my eyes drift to his lap, where he now has both hands gripped into fists on his thighs. I lift my eyes to his face. He's staring straight ahead, his eyebrows pulled down and a frown marring his face. I can see a nerve ticking in his jaw as if he is clenching and grinding his back teeth.

I glance over at Ana, who is writing with a slight smile curving her lips. I let my hand drop to my side and softly snap in her direction. Keeping my hand low, I point my thumb in Bryce's direction when she looks over. Ana leans back in her chair, stretching her arms over her head, and looks at Bryce. The smile slips from her face as she sees his rigid posture and expression.

Leaning forward, she mouths, "What happened?" while brushing her hand up and down her own arm. I roll my eyes. Of course, she noticed Bryce touching me. I shrug and mouth back "I don't know. Lunch." She nods, understanding.

The rest of the morning seems to drag on forever. Bryce has been avoiding me like the plague since first period. I think he might be schizophrenic. Or at least bi-polar. His mood swings are making me dizzy, and now I don't know if I even want to be friends...or more with him, anyway.

I sit down at our regular outdoor table to wait for Ana. I'm starving, but I can't bring myself to chance seeing Bryce in the cafeteria. It's bad enough I had to watch him hang all over Lanie Thompson and Amelia Boggs in second and third periods. He continuously flashed that killer smile at them while refusing to make eye contact with me at all. My only consolation is that he gave them the charming smile, the one that didn't quite reach his eyes, not the real one I've been on the receiving end of twice.

Suppressed

"Hey," Ana huffs as she sits down across from me. "Here."

She hands over a peanut butter and jelly sandwich, and I smile in thanks as I rip it open. The flavors explode on my tongue, and I moan in appreciation. "Thank you. I was starving."

"No worries. Now," she says, opening her own sandwich with delicate fingers, "tell me what happened."

I look around to make sure we're alone, then lean forward. I motion her to do the same. She rolls her eyes at me but complies. In whispered tones, I start talking.

"I have no idea. You saw. He was rubbing his thumb on my arm but, when I looked at him, he didn't even seem to realize he was doing it. I smiled and blushed, of course. That's when he pulled me in closer and told me he loves it when I blush."

I can feel the heat building in my face again as Ana smirks and says, "Nice. I told you he likes you!"

"Shh," I hiss, motioning for her to keep her voice down. "I might have agreed with you but not after what happened next. He tensed up, removed his arm and froze me out the rest of the morning."

"Maybe he..."

"See, you can't even come up with a valid reason," I say when her words trail off. "Ana, he went back to hanging all over Lanie and Amelia. I know you saw it too."

Ana nods. "Yes. I saw it, but I don't buy it. He looked like he was acting."

I say nothing to this. Sure, even I think those smiles he was beaming were fake. Maybe that's part of his game. Maybe he likes to draw girls in with his charm then break their hearts. Not that my heart is broken. I mean, I barely know the guy.

But I can't deny the twinge of disappointment I felt when he pulled away. If I'm being really honest, it was more than just a twinge. I'll never admit that out loud, though. Never. Bryce Howell will never know how his actions affect me, negatively or otherwise.

As if the thought conjured him, he's suddenly standing next the table waiting for Ana and I to acknowledge his presence. After one cursory glance to confirm it's him, I look back down at my sandwich without speaking. Out of the corner of my eye, I see Ana looking back and forth between us. She seems to make a decision, standing and stuffing the remains of her lunch into her sack.

"Hey Bryce," she says, as I shoot a tight-lipped look at her. She completely ignores it. "Sorry to eat and run, but I gotta go, uh, do...something. Bye!"

I watch incredulously as she practically runs away from the table. I shut my gaping mouth and look back down at my lap. The table shifts as Bryce lowers himself onto the bench Ana vacated. If I refuse to look at him, maybe he'll leave. He clears his throat. When I don't respond, or make eye contact, he does it again. I roll my eyes skyward before giving in and looking at him.

"What?" My voice comes out harsher than I intended. So much for not letting him know he'd hurt me.

He flinches, which makes me flinch in turn. When did I turn into such a harpy? I relax the muscles in my face, trying for an impassive look. I try again.

"How can I help you, Bryce?" I say in pleasant, even tones.

"Ouch, that one's even worse. I prefer your honesty."

"You want my honesty?" I ask, my voice rising in pitch and volume with each word. I lean forward and lower it so only he can hear me. "How about you be honest with me? You're so hot and cold, I never know which Bryce I'm going to get. What's the deal?"

"I want to tell you, Kai. Really, I do. I just...can't."

"Well, I guess we're done here," I say, rising from my seat.

"Wait. Please, sit back down." I comply, but I'm ready to bolt if he continues to put me off. "Thanks. I... okay. I'll tell you everything but not here. Can we meet at our spot after school?"

"Our spot? We don't have a spot."

He flashes a smile at me that seriously threatens to melt my bones. "Sure, we do. In the bushes where no one can see or hear us."

I nod and he gets up and walks away. I'm dumbfounded once again by his lack of courtesy. He could at least say goodbye. But my impatience with his rudeness is short lived. Anticipation soon overtakes the feeling. I'm going to meet him in our

Suppressed

spot after school. We have a spot. I can't help smiling as I watch him enter the cafeteria. Bryce Howell and I have a secret spot.

Wendi L. Wilson

Chapter 7

My face hurts. I've been fighting to keep the stupid grin off my face for the last two hours, but it's a losing battle. The muscles in my face are exhausted, never having been used this much before. I can't stop the smile from creeping back as I walk down the street toward home. But I'm not going home. I'm going to our spot.

I stop walking and peer into the bushes. I'm pretty sure this is where I pulled Bryce off the road. I step off the asphalt and pick my way through the foliage. Yes, this is definitely it. I head further in, coming to the clearing where I stopped this morning. It's empty.

A slight panic builds in my chest. What if it was a trick? What if he told me to meet him here, knowing I'd come, only to make fun of me for getting my hopes up? For being such a loser? He's probably with Lanie and Amelia now, laughing about what a sucker I am. I fight the burning behind my eyes and turn to leave.

I freeze, choking back the scream that tries to work its way up my throat. Bryce is there, standing so close, I get another strong whiff of citrus. I try to take a step back, but my heel catches on a tree root, and I start to teeter backwards. I'm going to fall on my butt right in front of Bryce Howell.

Before I complete that thought, strong arms wrap around me and pull me upright. I can feel his heat against every square inch of my torso as he tightens his grip, pulling me against him. I inhale, a combination of a shocked gasp and a pleasant deep breath that ends on a sigh.

The sound seems to jerk Bryce to his senses and he takes a step back, keeping his hands on my shoulders. "Are you okay?" he asks.

"Yeah. Thanks."

My words are stilted as I fight to control the emotion welling up inside me. I keep forgetting I'm supposed to be mad at him. We're supposed to be having a serious discussion about his wild mood swings. I'm supposed to be the one in control here, not Bryce. I shrug my shoulders. He takes the hint and releases his grip on me, letting his arms fall to his sides.

"Thanks for coming," he says.

I nod. "How did you get here? I didn't hear anything and suddenly you were behind me."

"It's...complicated, and part of what I have to tell you."

"Okay," I say, drawing the end of the word out like a question.

Bryce sits down on a bed of leaves at the base of a tree and pats the ground next to him. I want to be obstinate, to tell him I prefer to stand and that he should just get on with it, but I keep my mouth shut. I step close to him and sit, making sure to leave space between us. I can't think when he's too close, and I need my wits right now.

"Okay, Kai. I'll tell you everything, but you have to promise to keep an open mind and a closed mouth."

"I-"

He holds up a hand to cut me off. "I'm sorry. I shouldn't have said it like that. Can you please just let me get it all out before you speak? No interruptions?"

"Sure." I can't promise him anything, but I resolve to try.

"My family is...different. It's been drilled into me, for as long as I can remember, to never let anyone get too close. No ties. We move a lot, so it's actually a good thing that I never let anyone in. No one to miss. No hearts to break. I've lived this way my whole life."

I stare intently at him, soaking in his words. It makes me sad, though I understand the feeling. The only person I have besides my mom is Ana. But at least I have her. It sounds like Bryce hasn't ever had anyone.

"When we moved here," he continues, "I stuck to the same patterns I always have. Never talk to one person too much. Spread myself around, and when someone starts to get too close, brush them off with insults. Make them dislike me. I can't let anyone see the real me."

"But...why not?" The words rise unbidden to my tongue and are out before I can stop them.

Bryce gives me a pointed look, and I shake my head and mime locking my lips and throwing away an invisible key. That smile makes another appearance, and I can't help but smile back. He reaches between us and takes my hand, giving it a squeeze before releasing it.

"When I met you the morning of my first day, I... I don't know. There was something about you, something I couldn't resist. Something that made me want to draw you in. That's why I was so rude. I didn't know how to deal with the feelings you invoked. At that moment, I decided that my best, and only, course of action was to stay away from you altogether.

"I couldn't stick to it, though. I saw you swimming and was fascinated. Something pulled me down to the beach, like an invisible string drawing me to you. I felt like I had to talk to you, even if for just a moment."

He pauses to reach over and take my hand again, this time not letting go. His palm against mine feels like a branding iron, spreading heat and electric tingles all the way up to my shoulder. I lift my eyes to his, staring into the deep blue depths. I increase the pressure of my grip on his hand, silently encouraging him to continue.

"This morning, when you told me you weren't allowed to see me, something clicked in my head. My mind told me that the situation was perfect. If you're not allowed to see me, it makes things so much easier. But, Kai, my instincts rebelled at the very idea. It's unacceptable. I still feel drawn to you. I can't resist it anymore."

My heart swells at his words but shrivels nearly as quickly. There's a catch. He hasn't told me why he keeps everyone at arm's length. I have a feeling in my gut that I'm not going to like it.

"Just tell me," I say, unable to handle the silence for another second.

I see his adam's apple bob as he swallows thickly. Beads of sweat glitter on his brow, showing me a side of Bryce I haven't seen before. A nervous side. I almost change my mind and tell him not to tell me when he starts to speak.

"I have certain...abilities." He pauses for just a second, unsure if he should go on. I give him and encouraging nod. "I can sense people's emotions," he says, spitting it all out in a rush.

"What?"

"I have the power to tell what people are feeling."

My body gives a little involuntary jerk at the stress he puts on the word "power." I'm confused, and when I'm confused, I always blurt out whatever I'm thinking.

"What do you mean, power? Like a superpower?"

Suppressed

He doesn't answer me, just stares me down as if trying to exercise some kind of mind control over me to make me believe him. I feel a momentary shock of fear, which is quickly overrun by anger. Does he think I'm stupid or something? Like I'll just believe any outlandish garbage he tries to tell me? I jerk my hand from his and stand.

"Kai, please." He stands and reaches out to grasp my shoulders, but I take a quick step back before he can touch me. Dropping his hands to his sides, he says, "You promised you'd let me finish."

"Fine. Finish."

"I felt your attraction to me when we met, and it was almost as strong as mine to you. I could feel it rolling off of you in waves. That's why I was so rude to you. I had to nip those feelings, yours and mine, in the bud. I thought I had succeeded. I felt nothing but disdain from you after that.

"But then I watched you swim. Your joy was so absolute, it hit me in my gut, almost knocking me out of my chair. Sensing feelings from that distance is not normal, for me, at least. I couldn't resist. I had to go down to the beach. You drew me in like a beacon of light."

As I listen to his words, my disbelief starts to waver. A small niggling of doubt eats away at it. What if he's telling the truth? What if he really can sense things?

"After our talk this morning, when you told me you were forbidden to see or speak to me," he continues in a softer voice, "you were a jumble of emotions. I could sense disappointment, anger, rebellion, embarrassment...and at least a dozen more. Normally, all those feelings from one person would give me vertigo, spinning me in different directions. But from you, I felt each one individually and succinctly. Something about you brings clarity to the gift.

"Then I asked you why you were meeting me if it was forbidden, and your conviction hit me in the chest like a freight train. You refuse to let the old lady dictate your actions, yes, but there was something else there, too. Something I've never felt before. Something I can't really define. I'm sorry I jetted out of here like I did, but I needed to think. To process it all."

I begin to feel myself giving him the benefit of the doubt. I've heard of people having a sixth sense.

Suppressed

Maybe that's what this is. Or just a talent for reading people. That, I can believe.

"Is that all? Your parents don't want you getting close to anyone because you're really good at reading people? That doesn't make any sense, Bryce."

His shoulders droop. "I think you misunderstood. I'm not saying I'm good at reading people, Kai. I'm saying I can sense people's emotions. Every one. Like they're wearing a blinking neon sign."

"But...how?"

Bryce takes a deep breath and lays his palm on my cheek. Once again, his heat infuses me, making me feel safe and content. Like nothing can touch me. I'm invincible.

"I'm a witch."

"A w-"

I can't finish. My entire body flushes hot, then cold, and I throw his hand away from me. I take a quick step back, putting some much-needed space between us. My chest is heaving up and down, anger coursing through my veins like hot lava.

"Seriously?" I spit at him. "A witch? That's the best you can come up with? Is this some kind of joke? Are your little girlfriends hiding in the bushes, laughing at what a chump I am?"

I begin pacing, shaking my arms out at my sides. I'm so mad, I can't control the frenetic movements of my body. I want to scream. I want to cry. I want to punch Bryce Howell in the face. I turn and come to a halt. He's standing in my path, again without making a sound. Or maybe I just didn't hear it over the sound of my heartbeat pounding in my eardrums.

"Kai, please. I promised to tell you everything, and you promised to listen."

"That's when I thought you were being serious," I snap at him.

"I am being serious."

Something in his voice causes me to flinch. The words have a ring of truth. I feel the tension ease from my body in small increments. He really believes what he's saying. He really thinks he's a... a witch. A new feeling invades me. Pity.

As soon as I define the feeling, the muscles in Bryce's face tighten into a frown. "Don't do that," he says sternly. "Don't think of me like some head case that needs your sympathy."

"How did you..." My words trail off.

"You're not listening to me, Kai. I told you I can sense people's feelings. Your pity feels like a giant slug sliding down my throat."

"I..."

God, I don't know what to say. I turn my back to him so I can think. Either he's crazy or he's not. If he's not crazy, that means he really is a witch and...

"Do something."

"What?"

I turn to face him again. "If you're really a witch, prove it. Do something."

Bryce shoots a frown in my direction, obviously unhappy about my requirement of proof. He expects me to just take his word for it and believe he's a witch? Not a chance.

"Skepticism."

"Too obvious. Of course, I'm skeptical. You just told me you have magical powers. You said you have abilities." I stress the plurality of the word. "I've seen the emotion thing. Show me something else."

I hear a sigh before he starts to mumble something under his breath. I can't make out what he's saying, but the timbre of his voice affects me as a chill runs down my spine. I keep my eyes trained on him, listening to his mumbling and watching him move toward me. As he gets closer, I realize something's missing. There's no crunch of leaves or snapping of twigs. I look at his feet. I see a tree branch snap in half as he puts his weight down on it, but I hear nothing. As if to drive the point home, he raises his foot high and stomps it down. Silence.

"How did you do that?" The words come out like an accusation, but I can't help it.

Bryce sighs and rubs his forehead. "I told you, Kai. I'm a witch."

Chapter 8

I need time to think.

That's all I said before a ran away like a skittish deer. What I really want is to go for a swim, but the fear of him showing up on the beach again keeps me hidden in my bedroom. I don't know if he'd actually show up. He knows I can't be seen with him. But as my mom always says, it's better to be safe than sorry.

My entire body itches like I've broken out in hives. The wood floor is hard and unyielding beneath me, but the coolness of its surface seems to help with the itching. My brain is running in circles, and each rotation brings me back to the same point. Bryce Howell is a witch.

For the first time in my life, a boy has cracked my shell, wormed his way inside and made me feel something. Ana was right. I've never really even looked twice at a guy before Bryce. It's just my luck that he turns out to be some kind of freak of nature.

I sit up and lean my back against the side of my bed. I really wish I had a phone. I could use some advice from my best friend right about now. My face strains into a frown with the thought.

"I can't tell her."

The whispered words echo back at me. I can't tell anyone Bryce's secret, not even Ana. Regardless of how I feel about it, he trusted me. I have no idea how I'm going to pull this off. Ana can read me like a large-print book. I've never been able to keep anything from her. Maybe Bryce knows a spell...

I jump up and pace the floor. I can't believe myself. One second I don't know how I'm going to even look at him again and the next I'm wondering if he can put a spell on me to hide the truth. Guilt eats at me, and I'm not sure why. Maybe I feel it because I have to keep a secret from Ana. Maybe it's because I've been secretly meeting with Bryce despite my mother's dire warnings. Maybe it's because, in spite of everything, I want to be closer to him. I want to know him. I want him to know me.

I rush over to my closet and grab my swimsuit. I need to swim right now. If Bryce is stupid enough to come try to talk to me, I'll just ignore him. If Ms. Coraline sees me, she won't be able to find fault with me. I can't control his actions, only my reactions.

I tell myself all of this, even though I know the truth in my heart. If Bryce approaches me on the beach, it won't matter what I do. Ms. Coraline always searches for ways to punish or belittle me. It's just a chance I'll have to take. I don't think I've ever needed to feel the ocean around me more than I do right now.

As soon as my toes hit the surf, I feel like a weight has been lifted from my shoulders. Icy water splashes everywhere as I sprint through the shallow waves. As soon as I hit thigh-depth, I dive forward and swim under the surface until my empty lungs force me up for air. I tread water for a while, letting the sea soothe my troubled mind and body.

A strange feeling comes over me, like I'm being watched. I turn in the water and scan the beach, fearing the worst. I don't see Bryce, or anyone else for that matter, anywhere. I let my body relax and float on my back, staring up at the sky, it's blue color fading in the late afternoon light. The hair on my arms starts to prickle as I feel eyes on me again.

"It's probably just the old hag with her binoculars, again," I mumble.

As I try to ignore the feeling, it grows stronger, and I start to notice changes in my surroundings. The water has calmed, the large swells dissipating, leaving just a soft current to rock me gently. I close my eyes and enjoy the feeling, then pop them back open again. The water feels...warmer.

I turn myself upright and start to tread water again, looking in every direction. As I search for a logical reason behind the temperature change, the water steadily grows warmer and warmer until it feels like a hot spring, or what I imagine a hot spring would feel like. I straighten my arm and reach forward, jerking it back when I feel the shock of cold water just outside my personal space.

Something glittering in the sun catches my eye, and I turn toward Bryce's house. There, on the back deck, I see a lone figure leaning against the railing, sunlight glinting off mirrored sunglasses. I can tell it's him by his build and cocky stance. As I stare, he lifts his hand slightly in a wave, then wraps his arms around himself and shivers. He waves again and turns, heading through the double doors that lead into the house. As soon as

Suppressed

he disappears from sight, the water returns to its natural temperature.

A chill runs down my spine but not from the cooling of the water. I swim to the shore and run through the sand, barely slowing down to grab my towel. I take the stairs two at a time, needing to be back in the privacy of my room as quickly as possible. I pause at the back door, having enough sense to take a moment to dry off before heading inside. If I get caught dripping water on the floor again, I'll be in so much trouble.

After wrapping the towel around my waist, I reach for the doorknob. Before my fingers can brush the bronze metal, it turns, and the door swings open. Panic blooms in my chest, fearing the wrath of Ms. Coraline. Before I can make a choice between fight and flight, my mother steps into the opening and beckons me inside.

"Mom," I whisper on a sigh.

"Go, Kailani. Get to your room, now, and stay there. I'll bring dinner to you."

"But-"

"Now."

I swallow any further argument and do as she says. I head up the stairs to the third floor, my chest tight as I think about the look on my mom's face. It wasn't anger. It wasn't impatience. It was something far worse. It was fear.

Ms. Coraline must be on the warpath about something. Something serious, or my mom wouldn't have looked so apprehensive. As much as I want to sneak back downstairs and eavesdrop, I decide to err on the side of caution this time and stay put in my room like my mom told me to. Maybe she'll tell me what's going on when she brings my dinner.

After changing my clothes, I lay down on my bed. That whole scene with mom made me forget about Bryce momentarily, but as I lie down in the silence of my room, thoughts of him rush back in. I can still see him in my mind, standing on the back deck of his house, waving to me and making a shivering motion.

He did it. He used his...powers...to warm the water around me. He wanted to prove, if there was any doubt left in my mind, that he is a witch. I believe him. Bryce Howell is a witch. He can do things, out of the ordinary things, with his mind and his words. He can sense what I'm feeling.

I close my eyes with a flinch. It feels kind of ridiculous that, out of everything he revealed, the fact that he always knows what I'm feeling is what bothers me the most.

"Who cares if he can change the environment or prevent sound? He knows I like him." I whisper to the room at large, mocking myself.

God, I wish I could talk to Ana about this. I would even settle for asking my mom for advice- if it weren't for that whole "I'm forbidden to see him" bit. I have to keep all of this to myself. Unless I want to talk to Bryce about it. The thought sends a tremor through me.

"Kai?"

At the sound of my mom's voice, I sit up and scoot back, leaning against the wall. She walks in with a large tray and nudges the door softly with her foot until it closes. I keep silent as she walks toward the bed and sets the tray down in front of me. When I don't move, or speak, she crosses her arms over her chest.

"It's turkey and cheese on white. Your favorite."

"Thanks," I respond, still not moving to eat.

"Come on, Kai. You need to eat."

She moves around the room, tidying things here and there. I watch her with one raised eyebrow. Does she think I'll just let it go? No. She knows me better than that.

"Mom."

She turns to face me, her face looking a shade paler than usual. "Yes?"

"Come on, mom. What was going on earlier?"

"Oh, nothing, really. Ms. Coraline was on a rampage because I let her tea get cold, and I didn't want her taking it out on you."

"Really." I made my tone as sarcastic as I could manage.

"Yes, really. Now eat your dinner, and I'll come get the tray in a little while."

"I can bring it down to the kitchen."

"No! I mean...no, that's okay, Honey. I'll come get it. You can just hang out here and do homework or something."

"It's Friday. I don't have any homework."

Suppressed

"Kailani."

"Okay, fine. I'll stay here." I pause for a moment. "Mom? You know you can tell me the truth, right?"

Her shoulders sag at my words. "I know, Honey. I know." She walks through the door and closes it behind her with a soft click.

The turkey sandwich sticks to the roof of my mouth as I try to choke down a few bites. I drop it back to my plate and push the tray aside, gulping some water to aid its descent down my throat. Setting the glass back on my night stand, I lay back against my pillow and stare at the ceiling.

I wonder what's happening downstairs. It must be something bad if mom doesn't want me to leave my room. The old hag must be in a mood. I frown at the thought. I've seen Ms. Coraline in a bad mood. Hell, that's a daily occurrence. This must be something different. It has to be.

Making a decision, I grab the tray and tiptoe to my door. The metal knob feels unnaturally cold against my fingers as I grasp it and twist. I poke my head through the narrow opening and look both ways. All's quiet, so I step into the hall and make my way to the staircase.

I stick to the sides of the steps, hoping to avoid any creaking boards beneath the carpet. My back is sliding along the wall. I hear a noise and freeze, waiting for Ms. Coraline to pop out of the shadows and... I don't know what. When no one appears, I take a few more steps and hit the second story landing.

Muffled voices draw me forward. If I can't hear them clearly, that means they're behind closed doors, probably in Ms. Coraline's parlor. I rush down the steps as quickly as I can without letting the dishes on the tray rattle. One of the voices raises an octave, luring me to the closed parlor doors. Ms. Coraline is yelling.

"...Merryn. I know she has been seeing that boy."

"No, ma'am. I assure you, she's a good girl."

I flinch at my mother's words. I've always considered myself good. There's just something about Bryce that brings out my not so good side. And I like it.

"Don't be so naive. Kailani is..."

Suppressed

I press my ear against the doors as Ms. Coraline's voice fades. She must have moved further away. I can't make out many words, other than "young," "rebellious," and "pig-headed." I huff and feel my hackles rise with that last one.

"I've talked to her," my mom says, her voice pleading, "and she assured me she would stay away from him. She won't disobey me, ma'am."

Ms. Coraline's voice is louder when she speaks again. "You better hope so, Merryn. I don't make idle threats, so heed me now. If she tries to associate with him, even on a superficial level, I will pull my protection."

"Yes, ma'am."

My mom's voice is very close now, and I can visualize her backing toward the parlor doors. Change of plans. I know I'll never make it to the kitchen without her seeing me downstairs. She might figure out that I was eavesdropping. I sprint on the balls of my feet to the stairs, then take two at a time until I'm half way up to the second floor. I stop, get my breathing under control, then slowly make my way back down.

"Kailani!"

My mom's urgent, though not unexpected, whisper stops me in my tracks. "Oh, hey mom."

She rushes up and turns me around, leading me back upstairs. "I thought I told you to stay in your room. Why are you down here?"

"Sorry, Mom. I didn't really want the turkey sandwich. I was still starving, so I thought it would be okay if I came down to get some fruit."

She ushers me back to my room before speaking again. "Kai, I need you to listen to me. Ms. Coraline is...not feeling well, and I need you to stay up here. Please."

"Okay. Sorry," I say dumbly.

She pulls me in for a hug. "It's okay, baby. I'll take this tray down and bring you an apple, okay?"

"Thanks, mom."

Once the door closes behind her, I go to my window and stare out at the dark ocean. What did Ms. Coraline mean by protection? What could she possibly be protecting me from? And why does it hinge on me not associating with Bryce?

I walk to my bed and sit. I wonder if, somehow, the old lady knows about Bryce. About his abilities.

Suppressed

I shake my head at the thought. No way. How could she possibly know? She's just being her normal evil self, bent on making my life as joyless as possible.

"Well, I'm not going to let her anymore."

Wendi L. Wilson

Chapter 9

"I'm going for a walk into town."

My mom's spoon, laden with a heap of oatmeal, stops halfway to her mouth. She meets my eyes and nods before lifting it the rest of the way and taking a bite. She swallows thickly and takes a drink of her coffee.

"What are you going to do?" she asks, trying unsuccessfully to keep her voice casual.

"I'm meeting Ana. We're hanging out today."

Her relief is palpable. "Okay, Honey. Have fun and try to be back before dark."

I nod and jump up from the table. I grab my jacket from the hook by the door and rush out before she can change her mind and call me back. I pause on the deck and slip the jacket on, then slowly make my way across the weathered boards to the front of the house.

Stepping onto the driveway, I slow my steps. I don't really have plans with Ana. I feel bad lying to mom, but I need to see Bryce. I just haven't quite figured out how I'm going to make that happen. I can't exactly walk up to his front door and knock.

What if his parents tell my mom? Or worse, Ms. Coraline?

Once I reach the main road, I make a right and head in the direction of his house. My feet pick up speed, and by the time I reach the end of his drive, I'm practically running. I skid to stop and put my hands on my knees to catch my breath.

"What now?" I mumble.

I look back toward Ms. Coraline's house and see nothing out of the ordinary. I close my eyes, hoping a plan will come to me. When I open them, there he is, walking slowly up his drive toward me. My breath catches in my throat at the site of him, as if I'd conjured him. But I'm not the witch, he is.

I start walking again, pretending not to see him just in case the old hag has her binoculars out. I keep my head down and make sure my pace is quick enough that he won't catch up to me. At least, not yet. I can hear the sound of his shoes crunching on the gravel, so I know he's still there.

We walk all the way to town, me keeping my eyes forward, and Bryce trailing several yards behind me. I start to panic, wondering where to go and how this scenario is going to play out. I want to talk to him, to just be around him, but I need to make sure no one sees us. Ms. Coraline cannot find out.

Inspiration strikes, and I take a left on Fourth Street. As excitement fills me, my steps quicken, and I'm nearly sprinting by the time I reach my destination. I skid to a halt and look back. Seeing Bryce round the corner, I jerk my head toward the towering building in front of me. I wait for him to nod his head in agreement before skipping up the steps that lead to the entrance of the Santa Lorelei public library.

Walking through the doors, I take a look around and see that my hunch was right. It's pretty much deserted, save for a few people reading at tables or using one of the many computers. I pull the hood of my jacket up to cover my hair. Its bright color stands out like a beacon, and if there is anyone here who knows me, I don't want it drawing their attention. I head for the staircase and turn to see Bryce walking through the front door. I wait for his eyes to meet mine before turning and loping up the stairs.

Once on the second floor, I look around and sigh in relief. There's not a soul up here in the reference section. I hear Bryce's footsteps coming up behind me. I turn and give him a shaky smile. Relief floods me when he smiles back. Courage and determination, the likes of which I didn't know existed, flare within me. I reach forward and take his hand before turning and pulling him through the towering stacks toward the back. Chills shoot down my spine when he twists his hand and interlaces his fingers with mine. The heat of his palm sears mine, and I squeeze my fingers to bring it even closer.

When we reach the far side of the floor, I zig-zag through the aisles until I reach the most rarely used section. Rows of dusty, defunct encyclopedias fill the shelves. I found this spot when I was twelve. Ana and I decided to come here to explore one Saturday afternoon. We quickly grew bored, and I challenged her to a game of hide and seek. I hid in this section for over an hour before she finally found me. It's perfect.

"Encyclopedias?" he whispers, gazing at the shelves around us.

"Yeah. I don't know why they even keep these anymore. You can find anything and everything on the internet. No one should come back here. It's the best idea I could come up with."

He looks from the shelves to me and smiles. "This is great."

The bees start buzzing in my stomach again. Trying to act cool, I sit cross-legged on the floor and motion for him to join me. He plops down directly in front of me, crossing his legs so that his knees brush against mine. My breathing accelerates as I attempt, and fail, to calm my nerves.

"Why are you nervous?" he asks.

I meet his eyes with a sharp inhale. "I hate it when you do that." Ouch. Why did I say it like that?

He keeps the eye contact and speaks slowly. "I can't help it, Kai. It comes naturally to me and asking me not to do it is like asking me not to breathe."

I lean forward a fraction and take a deep breath. "I'm sorry. You just surprised me, is all. I'm still trying to get used to the fact that you can do it. I don't hate it."

He smiles at me, one that reaches his eyes and makes them sparkle like sapphires. I can't help but smile back. My whole body relaxes. For the first time, I feel totally at ease with him. I cock an eyebrow as a thought hits me.

"Are you doing something?"

"What do you mean?"

I motion between us. "I mean, are you doing," I lower my voice a notch, "a spell to make me more relaxed?"

Bryce chuckles and shakes his head. "No, I'm not doing anything."

"Can you do that?" I ask, my curiosity piqued.

He presses his lips together and nods. "I can. There are many spells that affect people's moods, their emotions, their desires." He shoots me a meaningful look as I flinch at that last one. "Kai, I promise I would never use a spell on you…unless you ask me to." He places his right hand over his heart and moves it in the shape of an X. "Cross my heart."

I see the truth in his eyes. "Okay. I believe you, Bryce."

Suppressed

"Okay, well, now that we have that settled, what are you going to do with me now that you have me here?"

I feel a stupid blush heating my face again. "I, uh," I stammer, "don't really know. I just felt like a had to see you."

The temperature of my face skyrockets. Why can't I keep my big mouth shut around him? I'm constantly blurting out whatever pops into my head. It's so embarrassing.

"Hey," he says, reaching over to place a hand on my knee, "don't be embarrassed. I wanted to see you, too."

"You did?"

He chuckles. "I followed you all the way here to this creepy corner of a deserted library."

A smile cracks my face. "You did, didn't you?"

"Yep."

"I overheard another conversation between my mom and Ms. Coraline last night."

"More forbidding you to see me?"

I nod. "Yeah, but it was weird. Ms. Coraline said something about removing her protection if I see you again."

"Protection? What does that mean?"

"I have no idea. My mom seemed really agitated about it. She tried her best to keep me in my room and away from Ms. Coraline, but I snuck out to listen. She kept promising the old hag that I would obey her."

"The old hag. I like it," he says, grinning.

I smile back. "That's what Ana and I call her. That, or the old wi-" I cut myself off quickly.

"Witch?"

The blush is back. "Sorry. I didn't mean…"

He shakes his head. "Don't worry about it. I'm used to it."

His words are meant to be reassuring, but I sense that I've offended him. I lean forward and roll onto my knees. Finding courage I didn't know I had inside me, I place my hands on his cheeks and stare directly into his eyes.

"I'm sorry, Bryce. Until yesterday, I didn't even know witches were real. All I had to go on was the wicked witch in the movies. I promise I'll never call her that again. She's not good enough to deserve that title."

I try to pull my hands away, but he slaps his against mine, trapping them on his face. He smiles and the bees in my stomach wake back up again. I'm starting to panic. I think he might want to kiss me, but I'm torn between wanting it and wanting to get to know him better first. I mean, he admitted that he spreads himself around to keep anyone from getting too close. What if today is just my turn on the carousel?

"Kailani."

The word yanks me out of my own head, and I refocus on his eyes. "Yes?"

He pulls my hands from his face but doesn't release them. "Stop worrying so much."

I huff out a laugh. "Is it that obvious?"

"You know I can feel emotions. When I am actually touching a person, it's amplified. I can almost taste your anxiety."

The word taste draws my eyes to his mouth. My tongue darts out to wet my dry lips. I wonder what his lips taste like. I've never kissed anyone before, but I bet he's good at it. The corners of his mouth turn up slightly. I jerk my eyes back to his and see humor shining in them.

"Oh, God," I whisper before shaking my hands free of his. If he felt my anxiety, he certainly felt my desire.

"Kai," he says, his voice low and smooth.

"No, it's...I have to go."

I plant one foot on the floor beneath me and push up, but my ascent is halted when he climbs to his knees in front me and grabs my shoulders. His stare snags mine, and I freeze, waiting to see what he'll do next. He gazes at me thoughtfully, then nods, like he's made his decision. I suck in a tremulous breath and hold it, waiting for him to speak.

"Kai, I..." He inhales deeply and blows the air out in a long stream, releasing my shoulders and letting his arms drop to his sides. "I don't know what's happening here. I'm not supposed to get close to anyone. You're not supposed to even look at me. Yet, here we are. I can't..." Another deep breath. "I can't stay away from you anymore."

Suppressed

The breath I've been holding rushes out, and I gasp for oxygen. I hear his voice but can't make out the words over the pounding of my heart ringing in my ears. I shake my head to clear it.

"Wh-what?"

"Are you okay? I mean, if this is too much, if it's not worth the risk, please just tell me. I understand."

"No!" The word comes out louder than I anticipated. "No," I say again in a much quieter voice. "I don't know what this is, either, but I think I want to find out."

Bright teeth flash as his mouth widens into that smile. My heart jumps into my throat at the sight of it. He leans forward and, in a panic, I turn my face to the side and close my eyes. I hear a slight chuckle and feel the soft brush of his lips against my cheek. His breath on my ear causes a shiver to travel down my spine and back up again.

"I can wait," he whispers.

When I open my eyes, I'm alone.

Wendi L. Wilson

Chapter 10

"Do your parents know about me?"

Bryce shakes his head, letting his gaze slip down to his feet. It's been a week since our first meeting here in the library. We tried to ignore each other all week at school, but it was hard...for me, at least. I still have a hard time reading him. There has been one big difference though. He stopped hanging all over Sandy, Amelia and Lanie. The thought makes me smile.

"That makes you happy?" Bryce asks, his face dropping in disappointment.

"What?" I ask, confused.

"I told you I've been keeping you a secret from my family, then I felt a rush of happiness from you. I thought you'd be more...disappointed about it."

"No," I say in a rush. "I was thinking about something else."

"What's that?"

Feeling the heat rise to my face, I shake my head vigorously and focus my vision on the dusty encyclopedias shelved behind him. I can't tell him the truth. I need to think of something else, quick.

The warm touch of his fingers on my chin disrupt my thoughts. My eyes fly to his, which are crinkled at the corners.

"Tell me."

I release my breath on a sigh and close my eyes. I don't want to lie to him. Opening my eyes, I steel my spine and blurt out, "I was thinking about how you've ignored the other girls at school all week," before dropping my eyelids closed again.

The touch of his hand amplifies with my eyes closed. His fingers drift from my chin upwards until his palm is flush with my cheek. I can't help but lean into it, rubbing my skin against his warm palm. I hear a soft chuckle and jerk away, my eyes flying open. I can't believe I just did that.

"Kai," he whispers, "don't." When I don't respond, he continues, "Please don't be embarrassed. I love your reactions...every one of them. Your emotions are so clear, so focused, it's like you're broadcasting them just for me. It makes me feel...I can't find words to describe it."

"Uh, we were talking about your parents?" I stutter, trying to change the subject.

Suppressed

Bryce leans back against the shelf behind him with a sigh. "Okay," he says on another sigh, "we'll talk about my parents. I've mentioned you casually. They saw me talking to you on the beach that night, and I told them I ran into you and introduced myself. That's all. They don't know we met here last week." He pauses and straightens his stance, his blue eyes shining. "They don't know we have a secret spot in the woods." He takes a small step forward. "They don't know I've met you there, to talk, every morning this week on our way to school...and every afternoon."

My heartrate accelerates and the bees start buzzing in my belly as he leans toward me. I try to keep my breathing steady and even. His predatory smile tells me it's no use. He doesn't need to rely on physical responses to know what I'm feeling. The thought causes the blood to rush hot through my veins, warming my face with yet another blush. He knows I want him.

"They don't know," he continues, his voice dropping to a whisper as his face comes within inches of mine, "that I'm here with you, right now, and that I've never wanted to kiss someone so badly in my entire life."

My heart leaps into my throat at his words. I can't seem to take a deep breath as the air whooshes in and out in shallow pants. He stares into my eyes for what seems like an eternity, waiting for...something. I'm not sure what. Maybe my permission? I don't know what to do. I've never done this before.

I open my mouth to say something- I'm not really sure what- but before any words can leave my lips he closes the gap between us and presses his against them. My eyelids slam down and warmth spreads across my chest as my heart tries to pound right out of it. His lips nibble a gentle rhythm against mine while his hands tangle into my hair. I start to teeter forward and brace my hands against his chest for balance. I can feel his heart pounding in time with my own. The realization that he's just as excited and nervous as I am makes me relax a little bit.

He must feel it, the tension easing out of my body, because a slight tug of my hair tilts my head to the side as he deepens the kiss. Of their own accord, my hands slip up over his shoulders and into his hair. I press forward, trying to get as close to him as possible. His right hand leaves my hair and wraps around my waist, pulling me toward him until our bodies are flush from the knees up. A moan works its way up my throat and escapes before I manage to smother it.

Bryce echoes the sound and tightens his hold on me. My body moves back as he pushes forward, until I am sandwiched between him and the bookshelf behind me. The hand on my back slowly descends, massaging as it goes, and I start to panic. I don't know what I'm doing. I don't know how far I should let this go and I don't know how to stop it...or if I *should* stop it.

Before I can finish the thought, Bryce's touch and heat are gone. I open my eyes to see him leaning against the opposite bookshelf. His eyes are closed, and his breathing is ragged. He has a pained look on his face that I think I somehow put there. I must have done something wrong. I know I somehow disappoi-

"Stop, Kai," he whispers, interrupting my thoughts.

Suddenly, he's in front of me again. His warm hands are on my cheeks as he tilts my face up toward his. He tucks my hair behind my ears before brushing his lips softly against mine once, then pulling back to gaze into my eyes.

"You didn't do anything wrong. You were," he says, pausing to lick his lips, "you *are* perfect."

"But-"

"No. No buts. It's my fault. I went a little...overboard." One side of his mouth lifts. "I just wanted to kiss you once, but when I had you in my arms, I lost all control. We were connected. I could feel you so clearly. Every emotion- your uncertainty, your acceptance," his voice deepens with each word, "your desire. No, don't be embarrassed. Please. I got so wrapped up in the feelings, that when you suddenly felt unsure, maybe even a little scared, it was a shock. I'm sorry if I came on too strong. I never want you to be afraid of me."

"Bryce." I swallow the lump in my throat and pull his hands from my face, holding them tightly in my own. "I wasn't afraid of you, I swear."

He's shaking his head before I even finish the sentence. "I felt it, Kai."

"Oh, God," I mumble. "You're going to make me say it, aren't you?"

Suppressed

"Say what?" he asks, raising his eyebrows.

Biting my lip, I take a deep breath, then blurt it out in a rush. "I've never done this before."

"What? Made out in a library?"

I squeeze my eyes shut and shake my head with a groan. "Any of it, anywhere."

"You mean, this was your first-"

"Yep," I cut in quickly before he can finish.

"No way."

I hear what sounds suspiciously like humor in his voice and snap my eyes open. "Are you laughing at me?" I ask, incredulous.

The smile drops from his face. "No! Never. I just can't believe no one has ever kissed you before. You're so...irresistible. I'm the king of resistance, and I never stood a chance."

The rock that had lodged itself into my chest started to dissolve. "Well, I've never been interested in anyone before," I say, injecting as much superiority as I can into my voice.

His teeth flash as the smile lights his face again. He pulls me forward and plants one soft kiss on my lips before wrapping his arms around me in a warm hug. "Until me?" he whispers, his mouth so close to my ear that his breath sends shivers down my spine.

Before I can reply, his body tenses, and he makes a quiet shushing sound. That's when I hear it. Footsteps. And they are coming toward us. I start to panic. If it's someone who knows us, or even just knows who I am, I'm in big trouble. I can't be seen with Bryce. I need to get away, but this aisle is attached to the back wall. There's nowhere to run.

Bryce releases me, takes a step away and faces the open end of the aisle. He starts mumbling something and, as his voice gets stronger, it becomes clear that he's chanting. His words are unfamiliar, but the hair on my arms stands on end as I feel something swirl around us. It feels electric. Powerful.

"Nobis indeprehensus; hostis caecus. Nobis indeprehensus; hostis caecus. Nobis indeprehensus; hostis caecus."

The footsteps get closer and on pure instinct, I step behind Bryce and bury my face between his shoulder blades. A shock ripples through me at the contact, causing me to jump back just as a woman rounds the corner and stops, looking toward us with a perplexed expression. Bryce is quiet now and turns his head to the side while bringing his index finger to his lips.

I stand still, frozen in fear. I recognize her. She's the reference librarian, Mrs. Ellis. I open my mouth to make some excuse, not really sure what to say, but before I can utter a sound, she turns and walks back the way she came. "I swear I heard something," I hear her mumble as her footsteps echo down the staircase.

I press my hand against my chest, letting out a harsh breath. Bryce turns toward me, taking a step closer, but I raise my hands to ward him off. I need a minute to think before I speak. I watch him as he puts his hands in his pockets and rocks back on his heels.

"She knows me," I say quietly. "She knows my *mother*." Bryce acknowledges the statement with a nod. "How did she not see us?"

Pulling his hands from his pockets, Bryce holds them out in a placating manner. He can obviously hear the barely controlled panic in my voice. He takes another small step forward, cautious as though he's approaching a wild animal.

"Kailani, please. Don't be afraid of me," he says, starting to sound a little panicked himself. "It's just a spell."

"A spell?" It's like he's speaking a different language. I can't comprehend what he's saying.

He moves forward another step. "Yes. I cast a spell to make us...invisible, I guess, is the best way to put it."

"Invisible?"

His feet bring him within touching distance, and he slowly reaches for my hand. Rubbing it between both of his, he explains, "We weren't *literally* invisible, but the spell sort of...clouded her vision. It made her eyes tell her brain that no one was here."

"It did?" God, I'm being so eloquent right now.

"Yeah," he says, pulling me into his embrace.

He runs his hands over my back, massaging away the tension. I relax into him, laying my cheek against his chest. We stand there, silent, for several moments before I pull back to look into his eyes.

"You're a witch."

A small grin tugs at the corner of his lips. "Yes."

"You're a witch, and you cast a spell to make us invisible."

"Yes."

"Huh," I say, before pressing back into him.

He tightens his arms around me, laying his cheek against the top of my head. "You're not going to tell me how awesome that was?"

A chuckle escapes before I can stop it. "Bryce, that was awesome."

"I know," he says with a laugh, squeezing me even tighter.

Wendi L. Wilson

Chapter 11

"How was your library date?"

"Shh, Ana!"

I glance around the cafeteria, making sure she didn't catch anyone's attention. We're stuck inside for lunch because it's pouring rain today. No one near us seems to have heard, but Bryce catches my eye from the other side of the crowded room. He's sitting with some guys from the football team, blending in as if he's been here for years. He raises his eyebrows in unspoken question, and I give a small shake of my head to let him know I'm all right. I don't understand how he can sense my anxiety when so many people's emotions have to be blaring at him right now.

Looking back at Ana, I lean forward and motion for her to do the same. "It was wonderful," I say, feeling a blush heating my cheeks.

"Why are you blushing?" she hisses excitedly.

I glance around again, making sure no one is paying attention. "He kissed me."

"What?!"

I straighten and squeeze my eyes shut as her voice seems to echo around the room. Opening them slowly, I notice several people nearby looking at us curiously for a moment before turning back to their own conversations. Bryce catches my eye once more. He has one eyebrow cocked and a knowing smile playing around the edges of his mouth. I close my eyes and sigh. I can't keep anything from him.

"Sorry," Ana says quietly, bringing my attention back to her. We bend low over the table once more, bringing our heads together. "Sorry, Chica. You just surprised me." She pauses for a moment before her teeth flash in a wide smile. "How was it?"

"It was...perfect. At least, until I started to freak out."

"Why did you freak out? What did he do?" she asks in a rush, her protective streak emerging.

"Nothing," I say quickly. "Calm down, mama bear." I shoot her a grin to let her know I appreciate her concern. "He said he wanted to kiss me so bad," I say, my voice taking on a dream-like quality. "I wanted it too, but I didn't know what to say or do. He must have understood, because he just...did it. He pulled me into his arms and kissed me. Ana, it was amazing."

"So, what made you freak out?"

"Things got a little, uh, heated, and I wasn't sure what I wanted or what to do. You know this was my first kiss." I wait for her to nod before continuing. "Well, he...I mean, *we* got a little carried away. Or, at least, it seemed like it to me. He backed me up against the bookshelf, and his hands started to wander down my back..." I raise my eyebrows and nod suggestively, hoping she'll get my point.

She gestures with her hand in a circle motion. "Yeah, I get it. Go on."

"Well, I must have tensed up or something," I say, feigning ignorance, "because he jumped away from me so fast I didn't even know what was happening. One second he was kissing me and the next? Poof. Three feet away, eyes squeezed shut and looking like he's in pain."

Ana barks out a short laugh. "He probably was."

I roll my eyes at her but can't control my smile. "Shut up, perv." I take a quick peek around to make sure we're still being ignored. No one seems to be paying any attention. "Anyway," I say pointedly, "I thought I had done it wrong or something. Don't you dare laugh!" She wipes the grin off her face and nods at me with mock earnestness. I shake my head with a grunt. "Do you want me to finish the story or not?"

"Yes. Please finish," she says, her sincerity real this time.

"Okay, so I thought I did something wrong, but he said he felt me tense up. He didn't want to do anything to upset me, or push me to go farther than I wanted."

"Well, that's refreshing. Most boys would keep pushing until you give in."

I raise an eyebrow at her and sit up straight. "And how would *you* know?"

"Oh. I, uh, read it in a book somewhere," she says, giving me the most innocent look she can muster.

"Uh, huh. To be revisited," I say, making a checkmark in the air with my finger. "I still haven't told you the worst part."

"What is it?"

"You know Mrs. Ellis? The librarian at the reference desk?" Ana nods. "Well, she almost caught us."

"What did you do?" Her voice is filled with anxiety.

"She turned around at the last minute and went back downstairs," I say, trying to keep my voice neutral. "We jetted out of there as soon as it was clear."

"That was close. Doesn't she know your mom?"

I nod. "Yeah, and I'm sure she would have mentioned seeing me with a boy in the encyclopedia section next time she saw her. I'd be so dead."

"Yeah, me too."

I smile. "Thanks for covering for me, Ana."

She waves my words away. "Of course. You'd do the same if the roles were reversed."

"Of course."

I chance another glance at Bryce. He's laughing at something one of the jocks said, and, as if he can feel my eyes on him, he turns toward me with a smile. I smile back, and he winks at me before turning back to his tablemates. When I look back at Ana, she's peering over her shoulder in his direction. She turns back to me, shaking her head.

"You two are so cute, it's disgusting," she says, her lips turned down as she dry heaves dramatically.

"Don't be jealous," I say, laughing, before someone else catches my eye.

Lanie Thompson, who's sitting two tables over, is staring at me, hard, with a frown marring her face. As soon as I notice, she turns to look at Bryce. I look too, but he's looking down at his food. My eyes flash back to Lanie, who slowly turns back to me, eyes narrowed and shaking her head in slow-motion.

I hold my breath as she grabs her tray and stands, then walks away, her back rigid. My eyes follow her to the trash bin where she dumps her lunch. She takes one last look at Bryce before stalking through the doorway that leads to the rest of the school. I look over at Ana. She turns to me with a worried look on her face. She saw Lanie too.

"She knows something is going on between me and Bryce," I say quietly.

"Yeah," Ana says, nodding slightly, "and that's not good."

"No, it's not."

***

"Hey, you."

With those words, Bryce straightens from the tree he was leaning against as I emerge from the woods into the clearing of our spot. My chest fills with joy at the sight of him. It's been two days since we were last alone. Two days since our first kiss. Heat sears through me with the thought.

"Hey," is all I can manage to stutter out.

He strides forward and catches me around the waist before swinging me around in a circle. My feet barely touch the ground before his seals his lips to mine. I grab his shoulders for support as my knees buckle. He chuckles and pulls his head back. His blue eyes sparkle with mischief, and I love it.

"Did I just make you weak in the knees?"

"Shut up," I say, trying to keep the smile from my face and failing miserably.

He laughs again and pulls me in for a quick hug before releasing me and taking a step back. I pull first one arm from the straps of my backpack, then the other and let it drop to the ground. I shrug my shoulders to ease the tension the heavy weight caused.

"You know," Bryce says as he walks around me and begins kneading the stiff muscles of my shoulders, "if I could walk you home, I'd carry that thing for you."

"Mmm," I say. My eyes drift shut with pleasure while I move my hair to the side to give him better access. "You would?"

I feel his breath on the back of my neck just before his lips touch the sensitive spot. A shiver runs down my spine. "Yes," he whispers, "of course."

His hands stop their ministrations, and he turns me around to face him. The spell is broken as reality crashes back in. He can't walk me home. We can't be seen together at all. I don't know how long either of us can go on like this.

"I'm sorry it has to be this way."

Suppressed

"I'm sorry too, but Kai, listen to me." He puts his hands on my cheeks and brings his face close to mine. "There's something...special between us. Something I can't explain. I told you I have never felt anyone's emotions as strongly as I feel yours. Today, in the cafeteria, with all those people, I could still feel you, like I feel you right now, just the two of us in this spot. We have a connection. Do you feel it, too?"

My eyes burn with his words, but I fight back the tears. Nodding, I choke out, "Yes."

"I want to fight for this. I've never felt this strongly about anyone before. I don't care if we have to hide. I don't care how hard it is. You are worth it. We are worth it."

His lips capture mine again, but this kiss feels different. Instead of the urgency I felt before, now there's nothing but sweet tenderness. He's sealing his vow with a kiss. Though the thought seems silly to me, I can't deny the truth of it. Bryce Howell really does care about me.

He pulls away and tugs my hand, pulling me toward the tree he was leaning against when I got here. We normally sit at the base of it, playing twenty questions or thumb wrestling or just talking. The ground is wet and muddy from the rain earlier, but before I can protest, he pulls a folding lounge chair from behind the tree.

"Where did that come from?" I ask as he unfolds and sets it up where we usually sit.

"I stashed it here yesterday," he says with a wink. "I was tired of sitting on the ground."

He takes a seat, leaning against the backrest and straddling the seat. He motions for me to sit between his legs. Unsure, I sit at the end, my legs hanging off one side. Bryce groans and shakes his head at me.

"What?" I ask.

In response, he grabs my arm and gently tugs it. Pulling me forward, he turns me so I'm cradled between his legs with my back resting against his chest. He wraps his arms around my waist and sighs contentedly.

"There. That's better, isn't it?"

"Sure," I mumble.

"Why are you so tense? You don't want to sit with me?"

I force myself to relax against him. "Sorry Bryce. Of course, I do. It's just...weird, I guess. I've never been this close to someone before."

"You're afraid I'm going to try to have my wicked way with you, aren't you?" he asks, tickling my sides.

I swat his hands away, laughing. "I *know* you're going to try," I joke, nudging him with my elbow before letting my head fall back to his shoulder.

We sit in silence for several minutes, Bryce's fingers splayed across my stomach. I lift my arm and glance at my watch. I've only got about five more minutes before I have to leave. If I'm not home by four o'clock, Mom will worry.

"Tell me about this," Bryce says, reaching up to tap the face. "Why do you wear a man's watch?"

"It was my dad's," I say, my voice subdued.

"Was?"

"Yeah. He left when I was a baby. I don't know why, and my mom refuses to talk about it. This is all I have of him."

I sit up and swing my legs over the side of the chair. "I have to go."

Bryce groans as I stand up. "Already?"

I just smile and run my fingers through my hair, trying to tame the mess it became while lying with Bryce. He rises from the chair and swats my hands away, taking over. I sigh with pleasure at the feel of his hands running through my hair.

"I don't know if I've ever seen anyone with this color of red hair before. It's so beautiful." he says.

"Thanks," I say, my face burning. "It's the same as my mom's."

He smiles. "Have I told you I love it when you blush?"

"I think so," I say, wrinkling my nose at him.

I turn and walk away, heading for my backpack. I'm jerked back as Bryce's arms snake around my waist and pull me against his chest. I can't suppress my laughter when he nuzzles my cheek, pecking quick kisses along my jaw to my neck. I twist in his grip to face him, wrapping my arms around his neck.

Finding courage I didn't know I had, I raise up onto my toes and press my lips against his. His arms tighten around me as he takes over, deepening the kiss before I can pull away. The kiss goes on for thirty seconds, or maybe thirty minutes, I'm not sure which, before he ends it with several gentle nibbles on my bottom lip.

He sets me away from him, taking a deep breath and shaking his head like he's trying to clear cobwebs. "Go," he growls, "now, before I change my mind and keep you here all night."

I grab my backpack from the ground and swing it over one shoulder. Shooting him a crooked grin, I waggle my fingers at him. "See you tomorrow?"

He nods. "Definitely."

I walk back to the road, turn left and head for home. I just hope I can get this stupid grin off my face before I get there, or Mom and Ms. Coraline will know, for sure, that I've been up to something.

Yep. That did it. Thinking of the old hag wipes the happiness right off my face. It always does.

Wendi L. Wilson

Chapter 12

"How was your day, Honey?"

I rapidly chew the forkful of lasagna I just shoveled into my mouth and swallow hard. I clear my throat loudly before saying, "Sorry. It was good. A normal day. How was yours?"

Mom shrugs. "The usual."

I bite my tongue, then take another bite of my dinner before I blurt out something nasty about her slaving all day for Ms. Coraline. Mom gives me a pointed look, telling me my efforts are for nothing. It's no secret, how I feel about our situation. I shrug and try to smile.

"Anyway," Mom says, pretending like our silent conversation never happened, "I'm going to finish cleaning up here, then I'm headed to bed. Do you need anything else?"

I shake my head and glance at my watch. It's only half past six. "Are you feeling okay, mom?"

"Of course, Sweetie. I'm just tired. I thought I'd lay in bed and read for a few hours."

"Won't Ms. Coraline need you for something?" I ask, not quite able to keep the bitterness out of my voice.

My mom ignores it this time. "Ms. Coraline is out for the evening."

"She is? Where'd she go?"

"Kailani."

"Okay, fine. It's none of my business. Do you care if I go for a swim?"

"It's getting dark. You know I don't like it when you're out this late."

"I'll be careful, Mom, I promise. And I won't stay out too long. Please?"

Mom walks over and ruffles my hair. "Fine. Just be safe, okay?"

"I will. Thanks, mom."

Mom takes my plate and shoos me from the kitchen when I offer to wash it. Taking the steps two at a time, I relish stomping as hard as I want and not having to worry about the old hag. I rush into my room and quickly change into my suit.

Suppressed

As soon as my feet hit the sand, my adrenaline starts pumping, and I run as fast as I can toward the surf. I slosh through the waves, barely getting to knee-depth before plunging headfirst under a breaker. I swim out, making sure I head slightly to the left as I go. When I resurface, I turn toward shore and smile. I'm right in front of Bryce's house.

I wonder if he can feel my happiness from inside. I concentrate on him, trying to send some kind of mental signal. Laughing at my own silliness, I flip over onto my back and float. The moon is full tonight, hanging huge and round over me.

A large splash breaks the silence, and I flip upright. Treading water, I can't believe my eyes. A dark head breaks the surface several yards away, and I see Bryce's face as he takes a deep breath and heads back under. I don't know whether to be happy or scared as hell that he's swimming out to me right now.

Before I can decide, he surfaces right in front of me. We stare at each other for a full minute before I break the spell. "Is the water warmer?"

He laughs. "Yeah, I cast an enchantment to make the water around me warm enough to survive. Seriously, I don't know how you stand it."

I smile at him for a second before sobering. "What are you doing here, Bryce? What if your parents see us?"

"Hey," he says, coming closer, "I would never take that risk. You're too important to me. They are out for the night. I'm home alone. I was just doing some homework when I felt it."

"Felt what?"

"I don't know how to explain it. I felt this pull, like there was a string tugging me to the window. When I looked out, I immediately saw you out here. I could feel your joy, like you were projecting it to me, or something. It was really weird."

I can't stop my lips from stretching into a smile. "I was."

"What do you mean?"

He huffs the question out between labored breaths. Treading water after the long swim out here is taking its toll on him. I feel invigorated, but I do this almost every day.

"Do you want to head in?"

He smiles at me and nods. "Yes, please."

Suppressed

"Race you!" I shout before diving under and propelling myself forward.

When my hands scrape the bottom, I stop and stand up. I turn to look for Bryce. He's still about twenty yards out, but coming in fast. I can't help but admire his strength. He was visibly winded out there, but he's swimming just as fast as he did on his way out.

"You cheated," he growls as soon as he gets his feet underneath him.

I shriek with laughter and run toward the shore, but running is not my strong suit, and he quickly gains on me. Before I realize what's happening, he sweeps me up into his arms and twirls me around. A shrill scream escapes my lips before I cut it off. Bryce senses my mood change and releases my legs, setting me back on my feet in the soft sand.

"What is it?"

I look over at my house and release a pent-up breath. We're far enough away that the tree line blocks the view of us, even from the upper floors. Bryce follows my line of sight and sighs.

"I'm sorry, Kai. I wasn't thinking. Do you think she saw us?"

I shake my head. "The old hag isn't home, but my mom is. She was going to bed when I came out, but her window faces the front of the house. I don't think she could see us here, even if she was on the back porch."

He takes my hand and pulls me forward. "Let's go sit on my deck. I have some dry towels, and I can get us a drink."

When we reach the deck, he leads me to a low chair and drapes a large, fluffy towel over my shoulders. "I'll be right back," he says before heading in through a sliding glass door.

I look around as I wait. I have a clear view of the ocean, but a low wall on each side of the deck blocks the view from the neighbors. Unless I'm standing, no one from my house would be able to see me. I relax back into the chair and watch the light of the moon play on the water.

"Here you go," Bryce says when he gets back, handing me a tall glass of iced water. Taking a seat in the chair beside me, he takes a sip of his own water before speaking. "What did you mean out there, that you did project your happiness to me?"

Suppressed

"I don't know, really. I was wondering if you could sense me from inside the house. I was just playing around. I focused on you, trying to send a mental signal. I realized I was being silly and stopped and then...there you were, swimming right for me."

"Huh."

"What? You don't think I was able to really use telepathy, do you?"

"I can see you're skeptical," he says drily.

"Well, it's...it's ridiculous. Telepathy isn't a real thing."

He raises one eyebrow. "Neither are witches."

My face drops, and I backpedal, "I didn't say th-"

"Stop," he says, cutting me off. "It's okay. I was only trying to prove a point. Before you met me, you thought witches were the stuff of fairy tales. I can sense emotions, which is, in a way, telepathic. How can you be so sure telepathy isn't real?"

"Well, even if it is real, I don't have it. Don't you think I'd know by now if I could do something like that?"

One side of his mouth lifts into a grin. "Maybe you only have it with me."

"Wow. Conceited, much?"

I don't know why this conversation is upsetting me so much. He's only joking, but I can't help but let it get to me. Maybe it's because I'm tired. Maybe it's because, despite what I say, I've always felt a little off. A little bit different from everyone else.

"Hey," he says softly, reaching over to take my hand. "You okay?"

"I'm sorry. I don't know what's wrong with me."

He takes the glass of water from my other hand and sets it down on the deck. Standing, he pulls me up from chair, then sits in it and pulls me down onto his lap. I sit sideways, draping my legs over the arm of the chair and press my face into his neck. Bryce rubs comforting circles around my back with one hand while the other rests on my hip.

"It's okay, Kai," he whispers. "Your reaction is totally understandable. Truthfully? I'm surprised you haven't freaked out before now."

I huff out a breath. "I am not freaking out."

He laughs, causing my body to shake with the rumble of his chest. "Okay. What do you call it then?"

I lift my head from his chest and stare into his eyes. "You *were* being conceited."

"Okay, I'll give you that." He pauses for a moment and stares at the water. After I lay my head back on his chest, he continues, "But what if I was right, Kai? What if, somehow, you and I have a...connection, of sorts? One that we don't have with anyone else?"

I don't answer. I don't think he was even really looking for an answer. I enjoy having his arms around me for a few more minutes before sitting up and climbing from his lap.

"I should go. My mom will think I drowned or something."

He snorts. "Not likely."

I laugh. "Okay, maybe she won't think I drowned, but she may come looking for me if she realizes I'm still out here."

He stands up and grabs my hand, yanking me forward. His other hand grabs my wet hair and uses it to guide my mouth to his. I can taste the salt from the ocean on his lips, and it tastes like heaven. He must sense my satisfaction, because he groans and kisses me even harder.

I reluctantly pull away from him. "I'm sorry. I really have to go."

He scrapes a palm down his face with a groan. "I know. I'll see you tomorrow morning at our spot?"

I smile and nod. "Yes, I'll be there."

He steps forward and kisses me again, this time making it short and sweet. "Sleep tight."

I pick my way down the steps and start running as soon as my feet hit the sand. I scoop up the towel I dropped on my way out and head for the house. Once inside, I release a pent-up breath. All's quiet. Mom must be in bed, and Ms. Coraline must still be out. She'd be breathing fire down my back if she was here.

I climb into bed after my shower and think of my conversation with Bryce. What if he was right? What if we do have some kind of telepathic connection? Maybe I should test it out. I feel stupid, but I'm going to drive myself crazy if I don't try.

Suppressed

 The first thing that pops into my head is bananas, so, with a shrug, I concentrate. I focus on Bryce and think "bananas, bananas, bananas," over and over again. At this point, I feel really ridiculous. And hungry. But I'm too tired to move, so I lay back and pull the covers up to my chin. My last thought before I drift to sleep is of Bryce swimming toward me in the moonlight.

Wendi L. Wilson

Chapter 13

"Is that a banana?"

I look at the fruit in my hand and nod. I grabbed it from the kitchen on my way out the door, wanting something quick and easy. Bryce's interest in it makes me smile, thinking of my experiment last night.

"Yeah," I say, leaning back against a tree. "It's what's for breakfast."

Bryce licks his lips. "Can I have it?"

I laugh. "How about if we share?" I peel one side.

"Deal."

"Didn't you eat breakfast?"

"I had some cereal," he says, licking his lips, "but I have been craving bananas since last night, and we don't have any in the house."

My hands freeze, and my mouth falls open. "Last night?"

Bryce snatches the banana from my hand and finishes peeling it. He breaks off half and hands the rest back to me. Taking a bite, he groans, letting his eyes fall shut.

"Bryce," I say, "focus. When did you start craving bananas?"

"I dunno," he says around another bite. "Maybe nine-thirty? I was watching TV, and the urge suddenly hit. I was so pissed when I searched the kitchen."

I hand him my half of the fruit when he finishes his and stares at mine with longing. He takes it with a nod and shoves it into his mouth.

"Was there a commercial about bananas or something?" I ask.

"No, I don't think so. Why?"

"Bryce," I say, grabbing his hands, "I tried something last night."

"What?"

"Well, you know how we were talking about projecting? Like, me, sending my emotions to you?"

"Yeah." His expression grows wary.

Suppressed

"I was thinking about it and wondering if maybe we do have some kind of telepathic or psychic connection. I decided to think of something really hard and tried to project it to you."

His mouth falls open for a second. "Bananas?" he asks, his voice nearly a whisper.

"Yeah," I say, nodding. When he doesn't respond, I ask, "Has anything like that ever happened to you, or anyone you know of?"

"No," he says. "Never. I could ask my parents but..."

"But they can't know about me," I finish for him.

We stand there silent, in our secret spot, holding hands for several moments. I stare at him, but his eyes are vacant, his mind somewhere else trying to come up with a viable explanation for our apparent connection. Finally, I lose patience.

"Well?"

"I don't know, Kai. This is all new to me, too." He grabs my wrist and turns it so he can see my watch. "We should probably get to school."

I nod. "Okay. I'll go first."

I turn to leave, but he tugs on my wrist to pull me back. My momentum takes me right into his arms. He kisses me, a sweet, soft peck, then hugs me against him.

"We'll figure this out, Kai."

"Together," I say, as I pull away and head back out toward the road.

As I step out of the woods, a black sedan pulls up beside me and stops. The back window rolls down, and I see Ms. Coraline's pinched face frowning at me. My insides explode into a writhing ball of panic. I send a silent prayer that Bryce stays put. If he shows himself, I'm dead.

"What are you doing?" she asks, her horrid voice cracking.

"Going to school," I say, keeping my expression as even as I can. I can't see her, but I know my mother is in the driver's seat.

"Why were you in the woods?"

"I, uh, ate a banana, and I went to throw the peel in the bushes."

"Really." It wasn't a question. The disbelief was written all over her face.

Suppressed

"Yes," I say simply, hoping to end this conversation and get her on her way as quickly as possible.

"Well, let's see it."

"See what?" I ask, confused.

"Let's see this supposed banana peel." Her face transforms, the evil shining through her self-satisfied smile.

Trying not to panic, I nod and turn towards the woods. If I head back to our spot to get the peel, the jig is up. It's way too deep in the woods to make my story plausible. I take a few steps forward, then pause in shock. The banana peel is a few feet ahead, lying on a bush.

"Thanks," I whisper, knowing Bryce is there somewhere, even though I can't see him.

I grab the peel and school my features before turning back to the car. I hold it up and wave it around so Ms. Coraline can see it before dropping it back where I got it. She shoots me a frown before rolling up the window. The car lurches forward, and I watch as it disappears up the road, heading toward town.

Once it's gone, I turn back to the trees. "Bryce?"

He materializes to my left, making my jump with a squeal. "Sorry," he says, a bright smile on his face.

I throw my arms around him. "Thank you so much! You saved me."

"Am I your hero now?" he asks, smirking.

"Yes, definitely" I say before the smile drops from my face. "We can't use this spot anymore. It's on her radar, and she'll be looking to bust me doing something illicit here."

"Illicit? I'm down for doing something illicit."

"Be serious," I laugh. "What are we going to do?"

"Don't worry," he says. "We'll find a new spot, and I can cast a spell to keep nosy old ladies far away from it."

"You can do that?"

"Of course," he says, turning me around and gently shoving me toward the road. "Now, get going or we'll be late for school."

Chapter 14

I can't believe she locked me in my room. I don't even know how she did it. There's no lock on my door, but no matter how much I push and pull, it won't budge. In frustration, I kick it hard.

"Mom!"

I rear back to kick it again but pause mid swing. I hear the patter of footsteps coming down the hall. I press my ear against the smooth wood and listen, holding my breath.

"Kai?"

"Mom, please open the door."

"I can't Honey. I'm sorry."

"Mom! Don't let her do this. It's insane!"

"Shh, Kailani. Please be quiet."

"I don't care if she hears me," I scream. "I. Want. Out."

"I'll talk to her, Kai. Just please stop yelling."

"What do you mean, you'll talk to her? This is crazy. I'm *your* daughter. Just let me out."

"I'll be back."

"Mom!"

She doesn't respond, and I press my ear against the door again. I hear her footsteps fading away. I kick the door once more before stalking over to my bed and throwing myself down onto it. I stare at the ceiling, thinking.

I have no idea why I've been imprisoned in what was once my haven. It's Friday, and the last time I had a run-in with the old hag was Tuesday morning when she saw me coming out of the woods. I've done my best to avoid her all week with much success.

Bryce found a new secret spot closer to school and showed it to me Tuesday afternoon. He assured me that it was spelled to ward off everyone except the two of us, making other people feel panicked and repelled if they get anywhere near it. We've been meeting there before and after school ever since, with none the wiser.

I got ready for school this morning after my chores, just like every other day, but when I went downstairs to leave, Ms. Coraline was waiting.

Suppressed

Without any explanation, she grabbed my wrist and dragged me back upstairs. She shoved me into my room and slammed the door shut. That was the last contact I've had with anyone all day until the exchange with my mom a few minutes ago. I check my watch. Seven fifty-three. I've been locked in here for over twelve hours.

My initial fear was that she somehow knew about me and Bryce, but after thinking about it, I decided she would have said something if that were the case. The only viable explanation I can come up with is that she's crazy. Clinically insane.

What upsets me even more about this situation is that my mom is doing nothing about it. She's so afraid of Ms. Coraline that she's letting this happen. I don't know if I'll ever be able to forgive her for this betrayal. If...*when* I get out of here, I'm going to let her have it. After I eat. I'm starving.

I sit up swiftly and stare at my door. I thought I heard...there it is again. A soft click is followed by a slight jiggle of the doorknob. I stay where I am, frozen, praying it's not the old hag. After another click, the knob turns, and my door swings open. I tilt my head to the side and squint. No one is there. I start to stand but fall back onto my butt when the door gently closes on its own.

Before I can panic, the air in front of the door shimmers. A solid form emerges, and I gulp back a scream as I realize it's Bryce. I jump to my feet and rush across the room. He pulls me in for a hug and squeezes me, hard.

"What? How?" I stutter when he releases me and takes a step back.

He holds a finger to his lips and pulls me to the far side of the room, away from the door. "I cast an invisibility spell and snuck up here. Why weren't you at school?"

My face tightens with anger. "The old hag locked me in here this morning."

"What? Why?"

I shrug. "I have no idea. She didn't say anything. She just pulled me up here and locked me in. My mom came by earlier and told me, *through the door,* that she would talk to her. She's my mother! She should let me out!"

My voice grows louder and louder with each word. Bryce calms me, placing his hands on my shoulders while making shushing sounds. I nod,

Suppressed

understanding. I have to keep it down or my mother or Ms. Coraline will hear and come investigate.

I pull Bryce to my bed and sit, pulling him down next to me. After we're settled I realize what I have done. The bees start buzzing in my belly again. I have Bryce, the boy I like, who likes me, on my bed. The thought is as terrifying as it is appealing.

"Relax," Bryce says, a wide grin on his face, "even if I wanted to take advantage of our current location, and make no mistake, I do, now is not the time. We have to figure out how to get you out of here."

"Wait, how did you know where I was?"

"When you didn't show up at our spot, I got worried. Then you weren't at school so I decided to make sure you were okay. I came through the trees between our houses and stayed just out of sight. I could feel you from there. You were angry, confused and..." he pauses to think for a moment, "hungry? Anyway, I made myself invisible and snuck in when your mom opened the door to sweep the dust out. I just followed the stream of your emotions and here I am."

"Huh." That's all I can come up with to say.

Bryce smiles and says, "Impressive?"

I smile back. "Very."

His smile drops. "Listen, my parents are out of town on business for the next two weeks. I-"

"And they left you home alone?" I interrupt.

"Yeah. They trust me and know I can take care of myself. If we can sneak you out of the house, you can come stay with me for a while until we figure this out."

"Stay with you?" I gulp. The thought of being alone with him in his house makes me nervous. "What about my mom? She'll never let me do that."

"Well, you can't stay here. That old lady is crazy. We'll just have to convince your mom that my house is safer for you. She could stay there too, if she wants."

My lips curve upward. "You'd do that?"

He nods. "Of course. I really care about you, Kai." His voice lowers with that last bit.

"You do?"

Suppressed

He doesn't answer. He just stares at me, his deep blue eyes shining with emotion. As I stare back, my eyes sting. I realize that I care deeply for him too. I don't know if I'd call it love, but whatever it is, it's strong. Really strong.

The emotion must be rolling off of me in waves, because Bryce closes his eyes with a shiver. They pop back open with what sounds almost like a growl. He reaches over and wraps his large hand behind my neck, pulling me forward. Our lips barely touch before we jerk apart at the sound of the door crashing open and slamming against the wall.

Fear envelopes me at the sight of Ms. Coraline standing in the doorway, heaving. Her face is twisted into a murderous sneer as she takes a couple of steps forward. Movement behind her catches my eye briefly. My mother is hovering out in the hallway.

"I knew it," she spits out. "I knew you were sneaking around behind my back, seeing that...that boy! You little slut..."

"Ma'am, please," my mother interjects as she slides into the room around Ms. Coraline. My upper lip curls. I can't believe she's calling the old hag 'ma'am' while she flings insults at me.

"Stay out of this, Merryn. I warned you. I warned you both."

I stand up, wanting to be on equal footing when she dishes out whatever punishment she's cooked up in her evil little mind. Bryce stands too, and pulls me behind him. Ms. Coraline laughs cruelly.

"Oh, what's this? Does the little witch think he can protect his inamorata from me?"

Three gasps echo each other at her words. Bryce backs up a step with a hand to his chest. I look from him to my mom, to see terror etched on her face. I'm sure my expression matches hers. Ms. Coraline just called Bryce a witch. She knows.

"Surprised, witch? Think *the old hag* didn't know about you, eh?"

I gasp again. How does she know what I call her behind her back? How does she know Bryce is a witch? What the hell is going on here? Bryce is still standing in front of me, and I hear him mumble something.

"Tsk. Tsk. None of that, now. Aborisci, Bryce Howell. Vehere domi. Imperio obsequendum."

Suppressed

Electricity races along my skin as I listen to her strange words. I hear Bryce's sharp intake of breath and reach out to touch his arm. I jump back with a yelp when my fingers brush empty air. He's gone.

"As for you," she says, taking a few steps forward. Her voice crackles with anger and something else. Power. I can feel it in my very bones, the power she's emanating. "You were told, nay, *ordered* to stay away from that boy! You dare defy me? Now, you must suffer the consequences."

"Coraline, no!"

I shift my attention to my mom. It's strange, I've never heard her speak to, or even of, Ms. Coraline without some form of respect or deference. The fact that she just called her by her first name alone scares me. Almost as bad as Ms. Coraline herself.

"It's too late, Merryn. She's had her chance. My protection is henceforth withdrawn."

"No! Please, ma'am." She slips back into her normal subservience. "Please give her…give *us* another chance."

"Mom," I say, finally finding my voice. "What's happening? What does she mean, protection?" *Where's Bryce*, my mind screams.

Mom just shakes her head at me and motions for me to be quiet. I look back at Ms. Coraline. She has a self-satisfied smile on her face. The smile doesn't quite reach her eyes though. Her dark irises look larger, almost swallowing the whites completely. She looks inhuman.

"What I mean, dear girl, is that I've been protecting you your whole life."

"Protecting me from what?" I ask firmly, trying to keep my voice from breaking.

"Never mind that. It's over."

She raises her hands into the air, and I feel power crackle through the room. I slink back until my butt hits the wall behind me. My breath is coming in short, fast puffs. I try to slow it, but it's no use. I can feel a panic attack coming on.

"Merryn, non hominom. Kailani, non hominom."

"Coraline, please. Stop," my mother wails.

Suppressed

"Syreni, ye were before. Syreni, ye shall be again. Reverto ad mare. Reverto ad mare. Reverto ad mare. Imperio obsequendum."

Severe cramps ravage my middle and I crumple to the floor, curling into a ball to alleviate the pain as much as possible. I crack my eyes open, biting back the scream trying to work its way out of my chest. I see my mother in the same fetal position, staring at me with tears streaking down her face. She mouths the words, "I love you," before climbing to her feet. Without another glance at me she runs from the room.

"Mom," I croak out, trying to call her back.

Ms. Coraline's laughter fills my ears. I cup my palms over them to try to drown out the sound. It doesn't work. I can feel the cackling reverberating down my spine.

"It is done," she says once the laughter winds down. "Get out of my house and never come back."

I climb to my feet and shuffle to the door, my back hunched over as the last remnants of the stomach cramps subside. I stop just over the threshold and straighten my spine. Ms. Coraline looks at me with one eyebrow arched, waiting to see what I'll do.

"Where is my mother?" I ask.

"She's home," she says.

"She's here, in the house, somewhere?" I ask, seeking clarification.

"No," she says. "Now get out."

Chapter 15

"Bryce? Are you in there?"

My knuckles are throbbing. I pound on the door for the fourth time and rattle the knob. I have no idea where he went when he disappeared, but I'd hoped he would be here. My body starts to shake as I remember him vanishing into thin air, followed a few minutes later by my mother. I squat in the shadows near the door and wrap my arms around myself. I'm alone. I don't know what to do. My breathing speeds up to match time with my heartbeat.

"Kai?"

I shoot to my feet, the near panic attack forgotten as Bryce trots around the corner of the house. I rush down the porch steps and fling myself into his arms. As soon as I feel his warmth against me, the torrent of emotions I'd been holding in floods out. My body convulses as I sob out my fear, my pain, and my frustration.

My crying eventually calms to a few sniffles and, once I can stand on my feet without his support, Bryce leads me back up the stairs to his front door.

He mumbles something under his breath, and I hear a clicking sound before the door swings open to reveal the interior of his house. All the details flow by in a blur as he leads me to the living room and sits me down on a large, comfortable sofa. He walks to a mini fridge in the corner and, pulling out a bottle of water, brings it back and hands it to me. He takes a seat next to me and wraps his arm around my shoulder.

"What happened?" he says, his voice soft and soothing.

I recount the series of events that occurred after he disappeared, ending with me fleeing the house. He listens without speaking, even when my voice cracks, and I have to pause to get myself back under control.

"So, I ran straight here. I banged on the door. Where were you?" I try to keep my words from sounding like an accusation, but I'm pretty sure they do anyway.

"When she cast that spell, I ended up here, locked in my bedroom. It took me a few minutes to work around her magic and get myself out, but when I did, I ran out the back door and headed for the tree line to cut back through to her house. I was halfway to her front door when I heard you, here, calling for me."

"She's a witch."

"Yes," he says, tightening his arm around me.

A thought occurs to me, and I inhale harshly. "My mother knew."

"What? How do you know?"

I stand and pace the room, shaking my head in disbelief. "She knew, Bryce. I overheard them talking. Ms. Coraline said she had me under her protection. She said if I defied her, she'd remove that protection. My mom served her like a slave..." My thoughts click from one to the next until the whole picture becomes obvious. I stop pacing and face Bryce. "My mom served her to pay for that protection. That has to be it, Bryce. Why else would she keep us in that terrible place? She always said we *needed* to be there."

Bryce doesn't respond. He knows I'm thinking out loud, that I need time to work it all out. He crosses his arms over his chest and waits, leaning back against the cushions of the sofa. My teeth chew my lower lip as my feet start moving again.

"Ms. Coraline is a witch. She cast a spell to protect me from…something, then held it over my mother's head and forced us to live as her servants. When she caught you in my room, she decided to withdraw her protection. I didn't understand her words, but I heard my name." I freeze and inhale sharply. "And my mom's name. Bryce, my mom was part of the spell too."

I walk over and sit down beside him. He wraps his arm around me, and I lean into his side. In whispered tones I say, "Why did she run away? Why did she leave me?"

"I don't know, Kai," he whispers back, "but I promise we will figure this out. I'm here, and I'm not going anywhere."

"What are we going to do?"

Bryce sits up and pulls me up with him. His grip is warm on my shoulders as he stares into my eyes. "We will figure out what the spell was, Kai. We will find your mom. She'll explain everything and together we'll fix it." His eyes are full of promise and determination, giving me hope.

"We'll figure it out," I repeat, trying to imbue truth into the words.

Suppressed

"Let's start with Ms. Coraline. Do you remember anything she said?"

I shake my head. "I don't know. It happened so fast, everything is a blur. After you disappeared, she said something about having protected me my whole life and that it's over now. She said my mom's name then something in another language. Then she said my name and repeated what she said after mom's. I just can't..."

"It's okay, Kai. Just relax and think. Anything can help."

My eyes widen as a memory niggles at the back of my mind. "In the middle of her spell, she switched to English. Something about...what we were before, we will be again. Does that make any sense?"

"Not yet," he says, biting his lip. "Every little bit helps. Can you remember anything else?"

"Only what I've already told you. She chanted something and pain exploded in my stomach and chest. My mom must have felt it too because she dropped at the same time. She told me she loves me and ran." I let me heart crumble a little bit more as I think of her leaving me with that witch to fend for myself. My back tenses. "Wait, I remember something else. Bryce, I asked Ms. Coraline where my mom went and she said *home.* When I asked if that meant if she was somewhere in the house, she said no."

"What could she have meant then?"

"I have no clue," I say slumping back down. "The more I remember, the more confused I get."

"Okay," Bryce says, standing and pulling me up with him, "that's enough for tonight. You have got to be exhausted. Let's go to bed. We'll start again tomorrow."

"O-okay," I stutter, suddenly nervous. Does he expect me to sleep with him, in his bed? I swallow hard.

Bryce takes my hand in his and leads me toward the staircase. He doesn't speak as we climb, only tightens his grip on my hand as my fear ratchets up with each step we take. When we get to the second floor he turns right and leads me down the hall to the door at the very end.

He stops before it, releasing my hand to turn the knob and swing the door open. He holds his arm out, motioning for me to precede him into the room. I look around in awe, my nerves momentarily forgotten. His room is gorgeous.

A large bed adorned with dark blue and brown coverings is centered on the wall opposite the door. There are nightstands on each side, each topped with lamps that glow softly when he flicks the light switch beside the door. The whole scene is set between two large windows which are covered with curtains in the same colors as the bedspread.

I walk over to one of the windows and pull the curtain aside. The ocean spreads out, dark and mysterious. It calls to me, making me wish I had my swimsuit so I could lose myself in its cold depths. I feel Bryce approach but keep my eyes on the sea. My nerve endings tingle as his heat seeps into my back.

"I got you some clothes." I turn to face him, pressing my back against the glass to keep space between us. He notices and takes a small step back. "The…uh…bathroom's over there," he says, pointing to his left toward a partially open door. "You can take a shower if you want."

I nod my thanks and take the bundle he holds out, then rush toward the bathroom. I close the door, trying to keep it from slamming it in my nervous state but failing. The loud pop of the door meeting its jamb echoes in my ears. I slump against it, forcing my quick, gasping breaths to slow by counting to four with each inhale and exhale.

I push away from the door with a groan. I turn and look at the handle, knitting my eyebrows. There's no lock. I stare at it for a few seconds, hoping one will magically appear, but it doesn't. I guess I'll just have to trust that Bryce will respect my privacy. A lock can't keep him out anyway. He's already proven that.

I examine the bundle of clothes he gave me. I set a red t-shirt on the counter and hold up the black sweatpants. They're big and baggy, but there's a drawstring. "This will work," I whisper.

I turn, excitement filling me at the prospect of a hot shower. I open the frosted glass door and sigh with pleasure. There are three showerheads, one gracing each wall of the enclosure. I turn the knob all the way to the left and close the door as cold water streams from the jets. Keeping my eye on the door, I slowly undress. I take off my watch and grip it tightly between my fingers for a moment before setting it on the counter.

Suppressed

Steam starts billowing over the shower door so I open it and adjust the knob to a comfortably hot temperature. I step inside and close the door behind me. The massaging jets feel glorious so I stand there for several minutes, letting the hot water soothe my tense muscles. I grab the bottle of shampoo and smell it before squeezing a large dollop into my hand. It smells like Bryce. I massage it into my scalp and rinse it out. A grab the matching bottle of conditioner and saturate the red strands with it.

Leaving the conditioner in, I squirt some body wash into my hands and lather my entire body, hoping to wash all the ugliness of tonight off of me. I scrub until my skin is pink then rinse it all off. I twist around to let the spray flow over my head, running my fingers through my hair to remove the tangles. I turn off the water and open the shower door. Cool air rushes in to kiss my body, causing me to shiver.

I grab two towels from a rack on the wall, wrapping one around my hair and the other around my torso. I wipe the steam from the mirror and stare at my reflection. My eyes are swollen and red, matching the color of my nose. I've always been an ugly crier and today is no exception.

"Kai?" Bryce's voice accompanies a light knock on the door.

"Yes?" I croak out.

"There's a new toothbrush in the medicine cabinet you can use."

"Thanks," I say, relieved he hasn't tried to open the door. "I'll be out in a minute."

I dress quickly, pulling the string on the pants and tying it as tightly as I can manage. I find the toothbrush and scrub my teeth with minty toothpaste. I pull the towel from my head and squeeze the excess water from my hair, then finger-comb it as best I can. I pluck my watch from the countertop and slip it into the pants pocket.

Taking a deep breath, I pull the door open and walk into the room looking for Bryce. His bedroom door swings open at that moment, and he walks in carrying a plate with two sandwiches balanced on top. He stops in his tracks when he notices me, his eyes drifting from my face to my feet and back up again.

Suppressed

"Oh, hey. I...uh...thought you might be hungry. Is turkey and cheese okay?"

I smile. "It's perfect, and I'm starving."

He returns my smile and walks to the bed, setting the plate down before climbing onto it and sitting cross-legged. When I don't move, he pats the spot beside him and waves me over. He picks up one of the sandwiches and takes a huge bite.

I force my feet to move. Making my way to the bed, I climb up and mimic his position. I pick up the other sandwich and take a bite. My eyes fall closed as the flavors burst on my tongue, and a small sigh escapes my chest. Bryce laughs, but I keep my eyes closed.

"Good?" he asks.

"Mmm hmm," I say, finally opening my eyes.

We eat in silence for a moment before Bryce clears his throat. "How was your shower?"

I don't know why that causes me to blush. "It was wonderful. I would kill to have a shower like that."

"Yeah, I, uh, could feel your pleasure."

"Oh."

The heat in my face multiplies exponentially. Bryce saying he could feel my pleasure brought a multitude of images to mind, all of them of the X-rated variety. Those thoughts brought my initial fear to the forefront. Where are we going to sleep?

"Hey," he says, pulling me from my thoughts. "What's wrong? You were blushing again, but now you're as white as a ghost."

"Nothing," I mumble.

"Kai. Talk to me."

I inhale deeply and release the breath on a sigh. "Okay, okay." I take another deep breath then spit out the words on the exhale. "Where are we going to sleep?"

Bryce's face lights up with a smile, the real one I love. "Here, of course," he says, rubbing his hand along the comforter.

"Bryce, I don't-"

"Kai," he interrupts, laying his hand on my knee, "listen to me. You have nothing to be nervous about. I would have to be some kind of ass to try anything with you now after everything that's happened."

"Okay," I say, not meeting his eyes.

"Hey, you believe me? Right?"

I raise my eyes to his and read the truth there. The truth I'm sure I knew all along. The tension flows out of me, and I nod. "Yes, I believe you."

"Good. But listen, Kai. I'm not leaving you in here alone. I can sleep on the floor if it will make you more comfortable, but I want to be here if you need me."

"No, it's okay. I trust you, Bryce."

He nods before getting up and setting the empty plate on his night stand. He grabs the covers and pulls them back exposing the soft, navy sheets underneath. He makes no move to climb in, only watches me to see what I'll do. I climb off and pull the covers down on my side before sliding back in.

Bryce slides under, too, scooting toward the middle. I roll to my side, facing away from him, and my fingers cling to the edge of the mattress. He pulls the covers over us with a sigh. A few tense moments pass before the silence is broken by his groan.

Suddenly, his arms are around my waist, and he's pulling me backwards. I tense, ready to fight or flee. He keeps pulling until my back is flush against his chest and his knees curve under my thighs. His body heat warms me, and I start to relax. The weight of his arm leaves my waist, and I feel his hand brushing my damp hair away from my neck. I shiver as first cool air, then warm lips brush against the sensitive skin there.

Bryce wraps his arm back around me and whispers, "Good night, Kailani."

"Good night, Bryce," I whisper back.

I lay there wide awake, listening to his breathing as the tempo slows and evens out. I try to concentrate on the sound, each inhale and subsequent exhale, but my mother's face kept intruding on my peace. The agony as she mouthed those three words before fleeing the room. I go over it again and again, trying to find some clue that I may have missed.

There is nothing else. She left me. That's my final thought before exhaustion takes over and my mind goes dark.

Chapter 16

"God, I'm so thirsty."

It's morning. I'm sitting at Bryce Howell's kitchen table, and he's cooking me breakfast. It's almost surreal how domestic it is. I've only known him for a few weeks yet here I am, sitting at his breakfast table after sleeping in his bed, *in his clothes* last night.

"Here," he says, breaking me out of my reverie.

I take the glass of water from his hand and chug it down, barely pausing to take a breath half way through. I don't think I've ever been this thirsty in my life. He takes the empty glass from me without a word and walks back to the fridge. I watch him pull a pitcher from the top shelf and pour icy water into the glass. My eyes focus on the condensation forming on the side, and I lick my lips.

"I wish I were this glass of water," Bryce says.

"What?" I ask, confused.

He chuckles as he walks over and hands me the glass. "You were projecting your feelings again."

"No, I wasn't," I say once I drain the glass.

"Uh, huh," Bryce says, walking back to the stove to flip the bacon. "Your desire for that water was stronger than anything I've ever felt from you."

"Hmm," I say, trying to coax the last drop out onto my tongue. "Can I have some more?"

Bryce nods and points his spatula at the fridge, inviting me to help myself. Finally, after finishing my third glass I feel satiated. I take the glass to the sink, looking for a sponge to wash it. Bryce taps the cabinet beneath the sink with his foot before heading to the fridge for the eggs. I find a sponge and the dish soap, then make short work of cleaning the glass before putting everything away.

"Thanks," he says. "My parents are sticklers for keeping everything neat and orderly so I do my best to clean up after myself."

"Where are they, anyway?" I ask, resuming my seat at the table.

"They went to Sacramento. There's a...family reunion, of sorts."

"Why didn't you go?"

Suppressed

He turns and leans a hip against the counter before pointing at me with the spatula. My face heats up, but the feeling is pleasant. He stayed home for me. I can't stop the smile that lifts the corners of my mouth. He smiles back before turning to the stove.

"I told them I didn't want to miss that much school, but they didn't buy it. I could feel their disbelief, but they accepted my choice and let me stay."

"Won't your family miss you?"

Bryce walks over, setting a plate of bacon and eggs in front of me before sitting down with his own plate. He takes a bite of bacon before answering, his eyes closing with pleasure. I shovel some eggs into my mouth. I didn't realize how hungry I was.

"It's not really family. It's sort of a meeting of our community. Several families of witches get together every November to socialize and perform rituals to bless the upcoming year."

"So, like a coven meeting?"

He points his fork at me. "Exactly. But Kai, when you meet my parents you have to pretend you think they've been at a family reunion. I'm not supposed to talk about this."

My fork stops midway between my plate and my mouth. "When I meet them?"

"Mmm hmm," he says around a mouthful of eggs.

I set my fork on my plate and clench my hands in my lap. "Are you sure that's a good idea? I mean, aren't you supposed to keep everyone at arm's length? Not let anyone get too close?"

The look he gives me is firm and sincere. "Yes. That's true, but I'm tired of keeping you a secret." He pauses to smile as a blush sears across my face. Again. "Besides, I'm going to have to explain your presence here."

"Do you think they'll kick me out?"

"No." He reaches across the table to take my hand. "Kai, they're good people. They may be a little pissed at me for breaking the rules, but they would never turn you out with nowhere to go. They can help us. I know they will."

"Can they sense emotions like you?"

He releases my hand and picks his fork back up. "No. Not all witches have extra-sensory abilities.

Suppressed

I'm kind of an anomaly. We've met witches who can read auras but none that *feel* everything the way I do."

"Do you think they'll be able to help us find my mom?"

"I don't know. We have two weeks until they get home. If we don't find her before then, we'll ask. In the meantime, we can search through their spell books and try to find anything that may help us."

I nod and resume eating, lost in my thoughts. I have no idea what's going on. I don't know where my mom ran off to or why she left me. I don't know what Ms. Coraline was protecting me from or what's going to happen now that I'm no longer under that protection. I look down at myself. I don't know what I'm going to wear. All my stuff is at the house, and I'm not supposed to go back there.

"Hey," Bryce says, pulling me from my thoughts, "don't let this consume you. We will figure it out. I promise."

"I believe you," I say, though I'm not really sure if it's true. "I was just thinking about my homeless situation."

"This is your home now."

I lift an eyebrow. "Let's wait and see what your parents have to say about that. Anyway, I was talking specifically about my stuff. You know, clothes, personal essentials, my backpack. How am I supposed to go to school without my books and notes?"

"You're really worried about school? With everything that's happened?"

"I know it sounds silly, but I'd miss it. Seeing…Ana! I need to talk to her. Do you have a phone I can borrow?"

He pulls a cell phone from his pocket and hands it to me. "Do you even know her number?"

I nod while tapping out the numbers on the screen. "I memorized it. I don't have a cell phone, and I'm not allowed to use the house phone, but Ana made me memorize her number. You know, just in case."

"Well, I'd say this is a just in case situation. I'll take care of the dishes. You can go out on the deck if you want some privacy."

I look from the screen to his face and smile. "Thanks, Bryce. You're the best."

Suppressed

As I stand up, he jumps from his chair and wraps his arms around my waist, pulling me close. The phone almost slips from my hand as his lips meet mine. He pulls back a fraction and says, "*You're* the best." He brushes his lips across mine once more before releasing me. "Tell Ana I said hi."

I walk out on the deck and close the sliding door behind me. Tapping the call button on the screen, I hold the phone to my ear and listen to the ringing tone. My weight shifts from one foot to the other while I mumble, "please, please, please," under my breath.

"Hello?"

"Ana? It's me. Kai."

"Kai?" She sounds a little bewildered. This is the first time I've ever talked to her on a phone. "Hey. Where were you yesterday? Whose phone are you calling from?"

"It's Bryce's."

"Oh. Okay. Did you guys meet at the library? Do you need me to cover for you?"

I experience a moment of panic when I realize I don't know what to tell her. I can't tell her Bryce is a witch. If I tell her Ms. Coraline is one, she'll never believe me. My mouth opens and closes several times.

"Kai? You there?"

"Yeah, sorry. I'm at Bryce's house."

All I hear is silence for a moment before she says, "What happened?" in a low voice.

"Ms. Coraline caught him in my room. He snuck over to make sure I was okay since I wasn't at school yesterday. She... She kicked me out."

"What?! What did your mom do?"

"She left. I'm not really sure where she went, but she said she would be back and that I could stay with Bryce while she's gone." The lie sticks to the roof of my mouth.

"That doesn't sound like her."

"Ana, I have to go. I promise, I'll explain everything later. I just wanted you to know where I was and that I'm okay."

"But-"

"Please, Ana."

"Okay," she says in a hurt voice. "I'll talk to you later."

Suppressed

"Okay. And Ana?"

"Yeah?"

"I love you."

"I love you too."

"Bye."

"Bye, Kai."

I end the call and wrap my arms around myself, unshed tears burning against the backs of my eyelids. I hate this. I hate lying to my best friend. I hate that my mother is missing. I hate not knowing what is happening to me. I press my eyelids together tighter as the hot tears start to escape.

Then, Bryce's strong arms are around me, pulling me back into his chest. I surrender to my tears and let them flow freely down my face. I look out at the wide ocean before me, wishing I could go for a swim. I know that would make me feel better. It would bring me peace and clarity. It would-

"Did you see that?" flies from my lips as something in the water catches my eye and cuts off my rambling thoughts.

"No. What was it?" Bryce asks, tightening his grip on me.

"Out there. In the water. I thought I saw something..."

"Maybe it was a dolphin," Bryce says when my words trail off.

"Maybe."

I say it but I don't mean it. It looked like a person. I scan the water over and over, but the morning sun is glinting off the waves, and I can't tell what is real and what is an illusion cast by the reflecting light.

The sound of a car breaks through my whirring mind, and I squirm out of Bryce's embrace. Rushing to the edge of the deck, I lean over and look toward the road. The sound is coming from the direction of Ms. Coraline's house. I listen carefully, unable to see anything through the trees. The roar of the engine grows fainter, but I can tell it's headed down the road into town.

I turn back to Bryce, who's looking at me with a strange expression, like maybe he thinks I'm not playing with a full deck. I shoot him a grin as I trot over and grab his hand.

Suppressed

"She's gone," I say pulling him toward the stairs that lead down to the beach. "Let's go get my stuff."

Wendi L. Wilson

Chapter 17

"That's so cool, how you opened the door," I say, shoving clothes into a duffel bag.

"She only locked it with the key when she left. I would have thought she'd put a ward on it too, knowing that I'm a witch, and I could get you in here."

I shrug, not really caring how she locked it. We are inside and that's all that matters. I walk over to my dresser and pull open the top drawer with a glance over my shoulder. Bryce is bent over, pulling shoes from the bottom of the closet, so I grab a handful of underwear from the drawer and shove them into the bag as fast as I can.

"Why are you embarrassed?" he asks. "They're just shoes."

"I'm not embarrassed." The words leave my mouth in a rush.

He takes a step toward me. "I felt it, Kai. And you're blushing again."

"Oh God."

I turn back to the dresser and shove the top drawer closed. I open the second one and pull out a few pairs of socks. Bryce seems to get the hint because he mumbles something about checking the driveway and leaves the room. I glance around. I think I have everything. We've packed two large bags full of clothes, accessories, and personal effects. I lift the other bag and carry them out into the hallway, closing the door behind me.

I grab my hair dryer, straightening iron and toiletries from the bathroom and head toward the staircase. I head down one flight and stop on the second floor, though, when I see the closed door to my mom's bedroom. The bags fall to the floor with a thud. I leave them where they land and walk over to the door, running my hand over the smooth wood before grasping the knob and turning. It won't budge.

"Bryce?" I call out.

"Yeah?" His voice echoes up from the bottom floor just before the sound of his footsteps.

"Can you open this?" I ask when he reaches me.

"Yeah."

Suppressed

He closes his eyes and mumbles a few words. The hair on my arms raises as the words fill the silence. I hear a click, and Bryce looks up at me with a smile. He turns the knob and pushes the door open before taking a step back.

"Thanks," I whisper.

Emotion rages through me as I step into my mother's room. It looks exactly as it did the last time I was in here. Nothing has changed. Yet everything has changed. She's gone, and I feel her absence in the pit of my stomach.

I look around, unable to figure out why I came in here. I walk to her bed and sit down. Grabbing a pillow, I press it against my face and inhale deeply. It smells like her. My eyes sting as I suck in a breath in an attempt to keep the tears at bay.

Dropping the pillow, I lean over and snatch open the drawer to her nightstand with more force than is actually necessarily. The light from the window glints off something inside. I reach in and gently pull out a silver locket attached to a chain.

I look over at Bryce, who's standing just inside the door. He gives me an encouraging smile. I look back at the necklace and turn it over in my hand.

Swirling letters are engraved on the back, but I can't make them out. I stand up and walk to the window and pull aside the curtain.

"What is it?" Bryce asks, coming up behind me and peering over my shoulder.

"It's a locket. There's something written on the back." I hold the locket up to the light, squinting to read the tiny writing. "It says, *My love is as boundless as the sea and stronger than any monsters that lie within.*"

I glance over my shoulder at Bryce before looking back at the locket. Slipping a fingernail into the crease, I pry it open. On the left, there's a picture of a small girl, maybe three years old. Bright red curls spring out from her head in all different directions as she laughs with closed eyes.

"That's me," I whisper, before letting my eyes trail over to the right side.

My breath catches in my throat, and the tears that were burning the backs of my eyelids earlier burst free. A smiling, handsome face stares back at me. Dark hair, square jaw, white teeth. Blue eyes. My eyes. *My father.*

"Kai? What is it? What's wrong?"

"She told me she didn't have a picture of him. She said she had nothing. Nothing but this watch." I run my fingers over the face. "She lied. I asked her...I just wanted to see what he looked like and she lied. She had this all along."

"I'm sure she had a reason."

His voice trails off. He knows his words are empty. His hand wraps over my shoulder and squeezes, attempting to knead the tension away. His touch jerks me from the dark place my mind had gone. I shake the anger away. I'm too tired to deal with it right now.

"We should go."

Bryce nods and slips his hand from my shoulder, trailing down my arm until it reaches my hand. He interlaces our fingers and pulls me away from the window. I shove the locket into my pocket and we leave the room, closing the door behind us. Bryce mumbles again, and I hear the lock click. He releases my hand and grabs my bags from the floor.

As we descend the stairs for what I know is the last time, I look around and try to dredge up some remorse...some nostalgic memory that will make me miss this place. Nothing comes to mind. We walk out the door, and I feel lighter. The unbearable weight that defined my life has been lifted.

***

"How was your nap?"

I smile and ruffle his hair as I pass the table where he's sitting and head straight for the refrigerator. Pulling open the door, I reach in and grab a sports drink from the top shelf. My fingers fumble as I try to twist the top off. I'm so thirsty, I feel like I may pass out before I can get the darn thing open. The lid pops free, and I press the bottle to my lips, tilting my head back and gulping half of it down in one shot.

Bryce chuckles, and I look at him, wiping my mouth with the back of my hand. "Sorry," I say, a little breathless. "I'm thirsty."

"Obviously," he says, smiling.

I shoot him a dirty look before taking another long swig of my drink. He laughs again. Barely repressing a smile, I shuffle closer and look at the book lying open in front of him on the table. There is writing on the pages, but I can't read any of it.

Suppressed

"What's this?"

Bryce wraps his arm around my waist and pulls me down into his lap. I stiffen for a moment, but as the heat of his body seeps into me, I start to relax into him. He presses a soft kiss to my temple before directing my attention back to the book.

"This is one of my parents' spell books. I was just looking for...anything that may help us."

"Find anything?"

"Not yet. I was hoping to come across some kind of locater spell. We could use your mom's locket to find her."

I mentally brush off the melancholy that tries to take over at the mention of that locket. I clear my throat. "You don't already know how to do that?"

The arm locked around my waist tightens briefly. "I'm here, Kai. Always." His whispered words reverberate through my body. "No," he says, the volume of his voice going back to a normal level, "I don't. I know a few basic spells to manipulate things around me, but a locator spell is complex. Every step needs to be completed with perfection and in the right order."

"So, you need to read the instructions," I say, the corner of my mouth lifting. "Never thought I'd hear a guy admit that."

"Ha. Ha."

I yelp and jump from his lap as his fingers squeeze my sides. Grabbing my drink from the table, I chug the rest of down and head to the sink to refill it. I don't know why I'm so thirsty. My throat is parched, and I feel the beginnings of a headache coming on.

"Do you have any aspirin?"

"What's wrong? Headache?" he asks, rising from his seat.

"Yeah. A little."

"There's a bottle in the bathroom. I'll get it for you."

He leaves the room, and I walk over to the table and sit in his chair. I slowly flip through the pages of the old tome he was reading. I don't understand most of the writing. It seems to be in Latin or some other ancient language. There are diagrams on each page that don't make any sense to me either.

Suppressed

Giving up, I push the book away and lay my temple against the cool marble of the table top. The pounding in my head is growing stronger. I squeeze my eyelids together and try to stifle a groan. Footsteps sound behind me, so I lift my head and crack one eye open to watch Bryce walk across the room.

"Hold out your hand," he says, twisting the top from the bottle.

I do as he says, and he shakes two pills into my hand. Popping them into my mouth, I take another long drag on my water and flush the pills down my throat. I set the bottle down and place my fingertips on my temples, rubbing them in a circular motion.

"Thanks," I croak out.

"Maybe you should go lie back down," he says, taking the chair next to me.

"I don't..." I trail off, gripping the sides of my head as the pain flares. "Maybe a hot shower will help."

"Of course," Bryce says. "Take as much time as you need. I'll be here reading if you need anything."

I nod my thanks and, dragging myself to my feet, I shuffle from the kitchen. I make my way to Bryce's room and rifle through my bags to find some clothes. My hand closes around a teal strap, and I yank, untangling it from the rest of the clothes haphazardly shoved into the bag. Holding it up in front of me, I can't repress the smile that stretches across my face. A swim sounds amazing. I can take a shower after.

I change into my swimsuit and rush from the room, my headache reduced to a dull throb beneath my excitement. I stop by the upstairs bathroom only long enough to grab a towel then skip down the stairs. I skid to a halt at the foot of the stairs and wrap the towel around my torso, covering my body from my armpits to my thighs.

I walk to the kitchen door and, shielding my body behind the wall, I lean over and peek my head through the opening. "Hey, Bryce, I'm going for a swim."

He looks up from his book and cocks an eyebrow at me. "Okay, but why are you hiding? I've seen you in a bathing suit before."

I shrug. "I'll see you later, okay?"

Suppressed

Bryce shakes his head with a chuckle. "See you later, Kai."

The thought of submerging myself in the ocean quickly pushes all others from my head. I feel a pull in my gut, an irresistible urge to dive in and let the sea swallow me. The ocean has always been my happy place, my refuge, but this feels different. It feels like I might...I don't know, explode if I don't jump in.

As soon as my toes hit the sand, I take off in a sprint toward the breaking waves. I reach the water line in less than ten seconds. Uncontrollable laughter erupts from my gut as the cold water splashes me. I run with high knees until the water swirls around my upper thighs. I cry out, a joyous shout that escapes before I can stop it as I dive forward and plunge head-first into the icy depths.

I swim for I don't know how long, until my lungs burn with the need for oxygen. My head breaks the surface, and I let the rest of my body float upward until I'm drifting with the tide on my back. There's nothing better than this. Enveloped by the cool, salty water, the afternoon sun shining on my face, the call of the sea birds. It's pure bliss.

The aspirin must have kicked in because my headache is gone. I feel amazing. I kick my legs down and spin around, treading water to gain my bearings. Bryce's house looks like a dollhouse on the shoreline, Ms. Coraline's sitting next to it just as small. I should get back. Bryce will be worried. I know he can't see me this far out. I wonder if he can feel my happiness from here.

I slowly head toward land, taking my time to draw the pleasure out as long as possible. There is a tingling feeling in my toes, but I ignore it. It's probably just the cold water. I take a deep breath and duck beneath the waves.

A school of large fish with bright yellow tails darts by in a flurry of bubbles. I head back to the surface with a smile. God, I love it out here. When I break the surface, I dunk my head back to slick my hair out of my face. I feel a frown pulling down my face as I realize the tingling in my toes has now moved up to encompass my feet and ankles.

I lunge forward, suddenly eager to leave the water. Something that feels like fear is driving me, an emotion I've never felt in the ocean. Never. I don't like it. I should fight it, swim in the opposite direction until it passes, but I continue toward shore. Something deep inside me is telling me I need to get out of the water. That this strange sensation in my feet is just a precursor to something larger. Something deadly.

I leave the water and trudge through the sand. Within seconds, the feeling is gone and so are my worries. I turn to look back at the waves. Shaking my head, I laugh.

"I'm so weird," I whisper to myself.

"Kai!"

I turn toward the sound and see Bryce rushing across the beach toward me, sand flying in every direction. I move in his direction, wondering what's happened. He pulls me into his arms as soon as he reaches me, his hands running up and down my back.

"What happened? Are you okay?"

"Bryce," I shout over his hurried questions. "Stop. I'm fine." I pull away from him to look into his eyes. "I'm fine," I repeat.

"You were terrified. I could feel it," he says, scrubbing a hand across his face.

"I'm sorry. I don't know…" I trail off, not really knowing how to explain.

"Kailani," he says softly, using my full name, "please. Tell me what happened."

I nod and slip my hand into his, leading him back toward his house. He stoops down and grabs my towel as we pass it. He releases my hand to drape it over my shoulders then interlaces his fingers through mine once more.

As we walk, I tell him everything. He listens without interrupting, his face thoughtful. "It was weird. I've never felt anything like that before," I finish.

"Never?"

I shake my head. "No. It was probably my imagination. Once I left the water, the tingling and the fear were both gone."

"Huh."

That's all he says and neither of us speaks again until we're back inside his house. I tell him that I want to take a shower and he nods, squeezes my hand before releasing it and heads back toward to kitchen. I pick my way up the stairs and head to his room to grab some clothes.

Suppressed

I see my father's watch on the bed where I left it when I changed. I don't know why I took it off. I always wear it, even when I swim. I pick it up and lay it on the night stand next to my mother's locket. Two mementos of two important people who are lost. It doesn't feel right to wear one and not the other so I leave them both there and head to the bathroom for my shower.

Wendi L. Wilson

Chapter 18

"What are you doing?"

"I'm getting ready for school."

"You're going to school?"

"Bryce, it's been nice hanging out here with you all weekend, but I can't just sit here anymore. I have to keep moving forward."

"But, I-"

"Stop," I say, pushing my fingers against his lips. "I just want to be...normal for a few hours. I am going to school. Besides, I need to see Ana. We can search through your spell books later, okay?"

"Okay," he says, slumping his shoulders, "but I'm going with you."

A smile tugs at my lips. "We can walk together. No more hiding."

He returns my smile. "No more hiding."

Yesterday, his parents called. He told them everything. They were upset at first that he'd gotten so close to me, but their anger at Ms. Coraline's actions against him overrode their misgivings about our relationship. They are now firmly on team Brylani. I laugh at the nickname.

"What's so funny?"

"Nothing," I say, grabbing his hand. "Let's go. We're going to be late."

It's kind of surreal, walking through the school parking lot holding hands with Bryce Howell. I see several sets of eyes skim past us and shoot back, widening. I try to keep my embarrassment at bay but fail miserably. Bryce squeezes my hand, and I look at him.

"Why are you embarrassed? Is it because of me?"

I tug his hand to pull him to a stop. "No, of course not," I say, my voice low. "It's just...nobody has ever looked at me before. Like, *really* looked at me." My eyes shoot from left to right. "They are all staring."

Bryce pulls me forward, wrapping his arms around me. I bury my face into his chest as he begins to speak. "Kai, there's nothing to be embarrassed about. Most of the girls are surprised to see us together, yes, but their feelings are positive. They're impressed. The guys are just jealous that I snatched you up before they even thought to try."

Suppressed

"Most of the girls?" I ask, afraid to know the answer.

Bryce snickers and nods to his left. "Well, there are a few who aren't very happy."

I lift my head from his chest and glance over. Lanie Thompson and Amelia Boggs are huddled nearby, heads together, eyes shooting daggers at me. Off to their right stands Sandy Evans, looking crestfallen. I can't stop the groan that works its way up my throat.

"Hey," Bryce whispers, pulling away so he can meet my eyes. "I feel bad for leading them on, but this is for the best. They know we're together, and I don't have to pretend anymore. They'll get over it."

He entwines his fingers through mine and starts walking toward the double doors that lead inside the building. As we pass Lanie and Amelia, I stare straight ahead, refusing to make eye contact with them. I don't need Bryce's ability to feel the hostility rolling off of them in waves.

"Slut," Lanie spits at me like the viper she is.

My breath catches in my throat. I've never been popular, but I've never been the object of such venom before either. Bryce tightens his grip on my hand and tries to pull me forward, but my feet have stopped and feel like lead. I don't know what to do. Should I fling insults back at her? Ignore her? Or just burst into tears?

Before I can decide, a familiar and welcoming voice rings out behind me. "Who are you calling a slut, Lanie Thompson? I heard you went upstairs with some strange dude from the mainland at Amelia's last party."

I turn back to see Ana, feet spread apart and hair whipping in the wind like some avenging angel hell-bent on seeking vengeance. Her narrowed eyes are pinned on Lanie, daring her to make a move or say something, anything. Lanie just stares back, face red with anger but silent.

I grab Ana's sleeve with my free hand and haul her forward. As she, Bryce, and I walk toward the steps I look over at Ana in awe. She has a self-satisfied smirk on her face. I shake my head in disbelief.

"That was awesome."

"Thanks," Ana responds to Bryce's statement. "Kai, are you okay?"

I nod. "Yeah. That was just...unexpected. Thanks for sticking up for me."

"Of course, Chica. I'll always have your back." She looks from me to Bryce to our joined hands. "So, you guys aren't hiding anymore?"

I can't hide my smile. "No. No more hiding. Ms. Coraline can't control me anymore, and Bryce told his parents yesterday."

"What do you mean? They didn't realize when you stayed at his house?"

"Uh, well, about that." I cast a glance at Bryce. "They're not home."

Ana's eyebrows shoot up into her hairline. "You guys are staying there, alone?"

Bryce chuckles as my face blooms with color. "It's not like that, Ana," I whisper furiously.

"Mmm hmm," is all she says before walking away to grab her book from her locker.

"Oh God," I mumble.

Bryce's laugh echoes through the hall, drawing more eyes to us. He doesn't seem to notice as he pulls me toward him and wraps his arms around my waist. His eyes sparkle with mischief as he lowers his face toward mine. I realize he's going to kiss me, right in front of all these students, just before his lips brush against mine.

Any embarrassment I might have experienced flies away as the pressure of his lips causes electric tingles to race down my spine. The students, the hallway...the whole school fades away and my mind goes blank. My whole world is Bryce. His lips. His arms wound tightly around me. His heartbeat pounding against mine.

Someone lets loose a loud whistle and the moment is shattered. I crash back into reality and hear students snickering all around me. I shoot a glare at Bryce, who is smiling like the cat that got the canary. At my scowl his smile widens even further, showing a row of even, white teeth.

"You did that on purpose," I say, my voice filled with accusation.

"Of course, I did. I don't know if you can accidentally kiss someone."

"You know what I meant," I say, some of the heat receding and being replaced by indignation.

The smile slips from his face. "Kai," he says, lowering his voice so none of the people lingering nearby can hear him, "I could feel their emotions. The doubt and disbelief from the girls. The challenge from the guys. I had to show them. We belong together. You know it and I know it. Now everyone else does too."

My anger deflates. The earnest look on his face is irresistible. There's no point in trying. I feel the corners of my mouth tug upward. My heart swells in my chest. Everything he does, he does for me. For us.

In this whole messed up situation, with witches and spells and missing parents, he's been my one constant. My rock. My savior. As I stand there, in the crowded hallway, swollen lips and pounding heart, I realize one thing. I love him. So much.

Bryce's eyes go wide and staggers back, one hand clutched to his chest. I lift a hand and take a step forward, but he shakes it off and straightens. A single tear trails down his cheek as he stares at me, his face filled with wonder.

"Bryce, what's wrong?"

"I've never felt anything like that before."

"Like what?"

I suddenly find myself being crushed against his chest. His hands are tangled in my hair and his lips are buried in my neck. Confused, I act on instinct and wrap my arms around his waist. His lips burn a trail up to my ear, and he whispers, "I love you too."

***

"When you come out, you come out in style."

Ana plops down on bench across the table from me. Opening her lunch sack, she pulls out two sandwiches and tosses me one. I nod my thanks and tear into it. She passes me a bottle a water and twisting off the cap, I drink half of it in one shot.

"Thirsty?"

"Yeah," I say, taking a deep breath after my long drink. "I don't know what's wrong with me. I have been drinking water by the gallons, and I'm still always thirsty."

"Huh. Anyway, you want to tell me about that little show you and Bryce put on in the hallway this morning?"

"What?" I ask, feigning innocence. "I don't know what you mean."

Suppressed

"Kailani!"

"Okay. Fine. Bryce wanted to make sure there was no question about our relationship."

"Oh, there's definitely no question. A lot of gossip but no doubt that the two of you are a couple."

I toy with the water cap, spinning it on the picnic table. The early afternoon sun warms my back as thoughts of Bryce do the same for my insides. My heart skips a beat as I think of his urgent words whispered against my ear in a thick voice.

"Bryce told me he loves me."

"What? He did?" I nod and she continues, "When? This morning?"

"Yes. In the hallway after he kissed me."

"Did you say it back?"

I smile. "Yes."

That isn't exactly the truth. I never said the words, but I must have been broadcasting my emotions. He felt it the second I realized I love him, so hard it knocked him backwards. At least, that's what I'm assuming happened. We haven't actually talked about it.

"Wow," Ana says, pulling me from my thoughts. "That's...amazing. I'm happy for you."

"Thanks."

Her face drops. "Have you heard from your mom?"

"No," I say, frowning.

"What exactly happened?"

"Ana, I want to tell you everything, and I will, just not here. Can you come to Bryce's house after school?"

"Yeah, I think so. Will Bryce be okay with that?"

"Okay with what?"

Bryce slides onto the bench next to me and stretches his arm across my shoulders. My face burns with a hot blush. I don't know how to act around him or what to say. His arm drops to my hip and he scoots me toward him, pressing his lips to my cheek.

"Okay with me coming over to your house after school."

"Um, I don't-"

"Bryce," I cut him off. "I need to talk to her. I need to tell her what's going on."

He stares at me hard. "Are you sure?"

"We can trust her. She's my best friend."

Ana's head swivels back and forth between us as we talk. "Are you in the witness protection program or something?"

"Something like that," Bryce says without taking his eyes from mine.

"Please."

Making a decision, he nods. "Okay. We'll tell her everything."

I smile and press my lips against his. "Thank you."

"Well, now I'm intrigued," Ana says, taking a bite of her sandwich.

I laugh and take another long swig of my water. I'm so blessed. I have the greatest best friend in the world, and I have Bryce. My boyfriend. Whom I love. Who loves me back. Despite all the terrible things that have happened, I feel lucky. And I have a feeling I'm going to need all the luck I can get.

Wendi L. Wilson

Chapter 19

"Are you high?"

"Ana-"

"Because you must be high," she says, not letting me get a word in edgewise, "if you think I'm going to believe this..." Pausing, she rolls her eyes to the ceiling. "Okay, *maybe* I could believe Ms. Coraline is a witch."

"Ana. Stop."

"No. I don't know what kind of con you two have going on here, but I don't buy it. And frankly, I'm a little pissed you're trying to rook me into it."

"Invisibilia."

I turn my head at the sound of Bryce's voice just in time to see him vanish. My heartbeat stutters even though I know the spell. It's the same one he used on us at the library. A gasp from my left draws my attention. Ana is as white as a ghost, staring at the chair Bryce was...is sitting in.

"Resurgo."

Ana's eyes bulge, and I look back toward Bryce, who has reappeared right where he was. He smiles at me and I return it, knowing that was just what Ana needed to lose her skepticism. I turn back to her.

"See? We're not making this up, Ana."

"B-but..."

"I know this must be a shock," Bryce says in calm, measured tones.

"That's the understatement of the year."

I can't restrain the grin pulling up the corners of my mouth. If Ana can make jokes that means she's coming around to the idea. She looks from Bryce to me and back again, then sighs and slumps back into her chair.

"Okay. I believe you. Start from the beginning and tell me everything."

"I've known for weeks that Bryce is a witch." I shoot her an apologetic smile for keeping that secret from her. "I couldn't tell you. I hope you understand."

"I do," she says.

Suppressed

"I knew Ms. Coraline was suspicious, especially after she caught me coming out of the woods that morning. She pretended like she bought my story, but now I'm sure she suspected I was out there with Bryce. I knew she'd be watching for me to go there again. That's why we moved our secret spot.

"Friday, when I was leaving for school she literally dragged me back up to my room and locked me in. I was stuck in there all day. Bryce used the spell he just showed you," I pause and smile at him, "to sneak into the house and come check on me. Ms. Coraline caught us together and went crazy."

"What did she do?" Ana asks.

"She called Bryce a witch. She already knew. She said a few words, and he disappeared."

"I was teleported here," Bryce adds.

"Then she argued with my mom, saying that she would no longer protect me. My mom got really upset, but Ms. Coraline wouldn't listen to her. She cast another spell, and my mom and I both hit the floor with stomach pain."

"So where is she now?"

"I have no idea. She told me she loves me then jumped up and ran from the room. I haven't seen her since."

"What? She just left you?"

I nod. "Yeah. I asked Ms. Coraline where she went, and she said she's home."

"Home? What does that mean? Is she still in that house?"

"I don't know. I asked the same question, but Ms. Coraline said no. Who knows if she's even telling the truth? Bryce and I snuck over there to get my stuff on Saturday and there was no sign of my mother. But I did find this."

I pull the locket from my pocket. I grabbed it from my room earlier, knowing Ana would want to see it. I dangle it in front of her, and she reaches out to take it from me. She opens it and stares at the pictures inside.

"Is this your dad?"

"Yes. At least, I'm assuming it is. He has my eyes."

"You were a cute baby," Ana says, snapping the locket closed. She flips it over in her hand and reads the inscription. "My love is as boundless as the sea and stronger than any monsters that lie within. That is beautiful, but what does it mean, monsters?"

I take the locket from her and read the back. "I don't know. I just assumed it was metaphorical. Like a knight slaying dragons for his love."

Ana sucks her bottom lip into her mouth and chews it. "Maybe."

"What, you think he meant literal sea monsters?"

Ana jumps to her feet and paces the length of the room. "Does that sound so crazy? You just told me Bryce and the old hag are both witches. Who's to say other...things don't exist?"

"I don't know, Ana." I say, looking to Bryce for help. "They are witches, sure, but they are still human."

Bryce nods, confirming my statement if there was any doubt. "Yeah," he says, "witches are human, but I guess in the grand scheme of things the existence of beings we don't know about isn't really that far-fetched."

I narrow my eyes at him, and he shrugs apologetically. I turn my attention back to Ana, who's stopped pacing and slumped back down into her chair. "Well, whether or not monsters are real, I still think it's a metaphor. It doesn't matter anyway. He left. His love obviously wasn't *that* strong."

I drop the locket on the coffee table, pushing away the melancholy that tries to engulf me. "Anyway, we've been trying to find a locator spell. We thought we could use that," I point at the jewelry, "to find my mother."

"My parents have all these books," Bryce adds, "but we haven't had any luck finding the right spell."

"Your parents are witches, too?" Ana asks. "Of course, they are," she says, not waiting for an answer. "What do they think of your current living situation?" she asks with an impish grin.

"They're fine with it," Bryce says. "It's weird because it's their rule that I not get close to anyone." He reaches for my hand and wraps his strong fingers around mine. "That's why I always sit with different people every day and don't let anyone in. Until Kai."

Suppressed

I smile at him, then look back at Ana. She's smiling, too. "But now they're like, yeah, go ahead and move a girl in?" she asks.

Bryce's face goes serious. "Not *a* girl. *The* girl." Warmth spreads through me at his words. He continues, "After I told them that old lady used her magic against me and hurt Kai, all bets were off. We don't use our magic to hurt people. Besides, Ms. Coraline kicked Kai out. I couldn't very well let her live on the streets, could I?"

"Is that the line you used on them?" Ana asks. At Bryce's smile, she says, "Nice."

"I haven't been able to get in touch with them since. I'm waiting for them to call me. When they do, I can ask them about the locator spell."

"Don't they have cell phones?"

"Yeah, but they're at a family reunion, and they tend to leave them off when they are there."

"That seems weird when you're home by yourself."

"They know I can take care of myself," he says, puffing out his chest.

Ana and I both laugh. There's a stilted silence for a few moments before Ana stands up and grabs her bag. Bryce and I stand up, too, and she hugs us in turn.

"Thanks for explaining everything to me," she says as we walk her to the door. "I have to get home, or my mom will send out a search party."

"I'll see you tomorrow," I say, hugging her again.

"Yep," she says. "Bye."

"Bye," Bryce and I say in unison.

She takes a few steps, then turns back. "Don't do anything I wouldn't do," she says, lifting her eyebrows suggestively.

"Shut up," I say, laughing.

With a little wave, she jogs down the steps and heads to her car. Bryce closes the door and leans back against it. He takes my hand and tugs me against him, wrapping an arm around my waist.

"That went well," he sighs.

"Yeah. Your disappearing act was genius. I don't think she would have believed us otherwise."

I take a step back and look into his eyes. "After going over everything that happened, one thing still bothers me."

"Only one?"

"Okay, a lot of things. But seriously, the catalyst for everything was our relationship. Ms. Coraline was adamant that we not have any contact. I wonder why that was. Why was it so important to her? I thought it was because she wanted to make me as miserable as possible, but her reaction was extreme. She outed herself as a witch, lost her live-in servants, and tore my mother and I apart. And for what? Because I disobeyed her and got a boyfriend?"

The corners of Bryce's mouth lift at that last word. He pulls me back into his arms, wrapping his arms around me and pressing my cheek to his chest. "We'll figure it out, Kai. We'll find your mom. I have a feeling she can explain everything."

"I hope you're right."

He kisses the top of my head and pulls away. "Come on," he says, interlacing his fingers through mine. "Let's go get a snack and do our homework like normal high school kids."

"Sounds great. I feel like I could drink a gallon of water right now."

He chuckles, pulling me into the kitchen. "You get the water, I'll get the food," he says.

I walk over to the fridge and grab two bottles from the door. Twisting the cap from one, I take a long drink. As I watch Bryce chop an apple into slices and slather peanut butter on them, my heart swells.

"Bryce," I say, waiting for him to look up at me. When he does, I say, "Thanks."

He seems to get that I'm not talking about the food. "Anything for you. Always."

Chapter 20

"Maybe you should go swimming."

I lift my arm from my eyes and crack one eye open to look at him. I've been lying on the couch since we got home from school, my head pounding and my throat scratchy. Without saying a word, I drop my arm back down and sigh.

"Come on, Kai. The last time you went in the water was, what? Saturday? That was five days ago. I know you miss it, and it made you feel better last time."

I pull myself up into a sitting position with a groan. Pressing the heels of my hands against my temples, I look up at him, silhouetted in the doorway.

"I know it did. At least, until I freaked out."

"Is that why you haven't gone back in? You're scared?" I start to shake my head, but he cuts in, "It is. I can feel it."

"Okay." I can hear the bitterness in my voice so I take a deep breath and start over. "Okay. You are right. I freaked out, and I'm scared it's going to happen again. But, Bryce, the ocean is my happy place. I don't think I could take it if it was ruined for me."

"I thought I was your happy place."

He says it with such a serious face, I almost believe he's offended. Then a nerve in his cheek ticks and the corner of his mouth lifts slightly, like he's trying to suppress a smile. I laugh despite the pain, and he chuckles in response.

"There's that smile I love so much."

I close my eyes with a whimper as pain sears through my temples. "Okay. I'll try," I concede.

"That's my girl. I'll go get your swimsuit so you can change down here."

"Thanks."

My head throbs with each beat of my heart as I wait for him. When I hear his footsteps jogging down the stairs, I ease myself up off the couch and take slow, measured steps toward the bathroom. Bryce meets me at the door and hands me my suit. Kissing my forehead, he backs up so I can close the door and change.

Suppressed

When I open the door, he's standing there in swim trunks, holding two towels. I lift one eyebrow and ask, "You're going in?"

"Ugh, no." He grins and hands me one of the towels. "I just want to be there, you know, just in case. If anything does happen I don't want you to be alone."

I smile. "You'd jump in and save me if I start to drown?"

"Ha. I don't think you could drown if you tried."

I wrap my arms around his waist, laying my aching head on his chest. "Thank you."

"For what?" he asks after I pull away.

"Everything."

He inclines his head and reaches for my hand. "Let's go."

The sand cools my feet, and the briny breeze feels wonderful against my face as we walk across the beach. The roar of the waves beckons me, and I pick up the pace despite the pounding in my head. Bryce chuckles and releases my hand as I break into a run.

Wendi L. Wilson

The water swirls around me as I wade out, making me feel more alive than I have in days. By the time I reach waist-depth and dive forward, the pain in my head is gone. I swim beneath the surface for several seconds then come up for air. I could have gone a lot farther, but the strange feeling I got last time is still fresh in my mind. I decide to play it safe and stay closer to shore.

Turning north, I swim parallel to the beach, my muscles stretching gloriously. I only swim for about a half a mile, then stop to tread water and take inventory of my body. My head is clear and pain-free, my throat has lost its persistent dryness, and I feel completely revitalized. It's strange that a swim in the ocean has healed all my ailments, but I'm not going to dwell on it. I'm just going to live in the moment and make the most of it.

I turn to swim back, but before I can dive under, movement to my left catches my eye. A wave crests and blocks my view. When it passes, whatever I saw is gone. I dog paddle for a few minutes, watching the water around me. I'm nervous, a sensation I'm not used to feeling in the water. I laugh at myself, trying to push the feeling away.

Suppressed

I strike out in a breaststroke, but my tempo flounders when I see it again. Closer this time, a dark object breaks the surface for a moment before ducking back under. Treading water, I stare at the spot. Nothing appears. I take a deep breath and prepare to dive under when I hear a splash directly behind me.

"Kailani."

I twist around in a panic and come face to face with my mother.

"Mom?"

"Hey, baby."

"Mom?" I repeat. My mind goes blank. I can't believe what I'm seeing.

"It's me, Kai."

Tears sting my eyes and I lunge forward, needing to touch her, to make sure she's real. My fingers barely brush against her hair before she jerks back in the water just out of reach. My throat swells until I can barely breath. I don't know what's happening right now.

"Mom, what's wrong? Where have you been?"

"I'm so sorry, Kai. I'm sorry I left you, but I had to."

"You had to?" Anger starts to push away the other emotions. "What do you mean, you had to? Mom, please, tell me what's going on."

Her eyes flood with tears, but she maintains her distance as she speaks. "I don't know where to start." When I remain silent, she takes a deep breath and continues. "As you probably know, Coraline is a witch."

"Yes, I figured that out." I can't keep the sarcasm from my voice.

"When you were a baby, she cast a spell on us. It was for your protection. There are...people who want to hurt you because of who your father is."

"My father? What does he have to do with this?"

She closes her eyes and scrubs a hand across her face. "Okay, listen, Kai. We don't have a lot of time. You have to get out of the water as soon as I leave. Promise me, Kai."

"What? You're leaving again? Why?"

"I'll explain, but you have to promise me."

"Okay," I yell, my frustration peaking. "I promise."

Suppressed

"As soon as I leave?"

"Yes!"

She inhales deeply, looking up at the sky. She moves her gaze back to me, smiling tentatively before lying back and floating on the surface of the water. I open my mouth to ask what she's doing, but no sound comes out. My jaw drops even further as a large, turquoise fish tail flips up out of the water and splashes back down.

"What the..."

I push myself backward in the water, trying to get away from the strange appendage. It disappears beneath the waves, and I stare incredulously at my mother's face. She smiles at me, her face sad, while I process what I just saw.

"What was that?" is all I can manage to spit out.

"Kailani, I'm a mermaid."

"A what?"

"Kai, I know this is a surprise, to say the least, but I need you to listen to me."

I nod but can't manage to speak. I think I'm in shock. My mother has a tail. She's a freaking fish. I can't believe it. I must be dreaming. I pinch my thigh beneath the water, hoping it will wake me up.

"Are your legs tingling yet?"

"What?" That seems to be the only word I can say.

"Focus, Kai." Her voice grows harsh. "This is important. Are your legs tingling?"

"Um, no. Not right now. I felt it the other day, though."

"Okay, good. If you start to feel it, you have to leave the water immediately. Okay?"

"Okay." I draw the end of the word out like a question.

"Kai, I'm so sorry this is happening."

"What *is* happening, mom?"

"We don't have a lot of time, but I'll explain as much as I can. You'll tell me if you start to feel the tingling?"

"Yes. Please just tell me."

"Okay. I was born in the sea…a mermaid. When I was sixteen, I met your father. He was a fisherman. A human. We fell in love, and I asked a

Suppressed

witch to turn me into a human so I could be with him."

"Ms. Coraline?"

She nods. "We made a deal. She would give me legs, make me human, but I would owe her a favor. One which she could collect on at any time." She pauses and sucks in a deep breath. "We were so happy when you were born. You were so beautiful, so perfect."

She smiles. "You still are. We lived in your father's family home. You know it as the old McCormick house. It belonged to his mother's family for decades. Mr. McCormick was your dad's maternal grandfather."

Chills run down my spine and I shiver. Mom sends me a concerned look, but I brush it off. "No, no tingling yet."

"One day," she continues, "when you were a toddler, you were splashing in the water when a riptide pulled you under and out. Your father and I jumped in and swam after you, but by the time we reached you, you had changed. You had a beautiful lavender tail."

"What?" I interject.

She continues as if she didn't hear me, her eyes vacant. "We didn't know. We thought you'd taken after your father and were human. We panicked." Her eyes focus and she looks at me, pleading for understanding. "Marrying a human is frowned upon in my home. Offspring between merpeople and humans is...illegal is the best term for it. You can never go there. They consider you an abomination and will kill you."

A tingling starts in my toes but I hold my tongue. I can't leave now. I have to know more. "I have legs now. What happened?"

"We took you to Coraline who, by that point, had moved in next door. It made her happy to lord over me that I still owed her. She agreed to cast the same spell on you that she had on me, to suppress the mermaid side of you, but there was a price. A steep one."

The tingling moves up my feet, but I ignore it. "What was the price?"

My mom's eyes fill with tears. "I had to give up your father. She would make you human but only if she could make him a merman and send him into the sea, away from us. Forever."

Suppressed

"No," I moan out, horrified. "How could she..." But I know the answer to that. Just like that tiny black kitten, she cast him into the sea to make us miserable for her own perverse pleasure. "Where is he now?"

"He's in my home, Delmare. I found him when Coraline reversed the spell, and I returned to the sea. He's been a prisoner there for the last fourteen years."

"That's why you ran out." It's a statement, not a question.

She answers anyway. "Yes. I had to get to the water before my legs changed or I would have died. I didn't want to leave you."

The tingling strengthens, and moves up past my ankles. I groan with discomfort and despite the sound of the waves lapping around us, my mother hears it. She closes the gap between us and places her hands on my cheeks. The tip of her tailfin brushes against my shin, and I shiver.

"It's happening?" I nod. "Kai, get out of the water now. Swim as fast as you can, straight for shore."

"But, mom-"

"Now, Kailani! Your tail is trying to form. If it does, you'll be stuck out here. They'll kill you. Go!"

"Kai!"

I hear the faint call from behind me and turn to see Bryce pacing up and down the shoreline, waving at me. When I turn back, my mother is gone. The tingling is moving up my calves, so I strike out for shore like the devil is after me. It doesn't take long to reach, and once I'm lying on the sand the tingling recedes.

"What happened?" Bryce asks, his voice laced with panic. "Your emotions were all over the place and it took me forever to find you."

"It was her," I say, tears pouring from my eyes as I scan the horizon, looking for any sign of her.

"Who?" he asks, plopping down on the sand beside me.

"My mother."

Chapter 21

I don't want to tell Bryce. I promised him I would, but as the hot shower beats against my back, I try to think of a way to get out of explaining. What if he looks at me differently? Who am I kidding? Of course, he's going to look at me differently. My worst fear is that if he finds out I'm not really human, he won't want me anymore.

I turn the spray off and step out of the shower, wrapping a large, fluffy towel around my torso. Wiping the steam from the mirror, I stare at my reflection. I don't look any different. If I don't tell him, Bryce won't know that everything has changed. I flash a bright smile at my reflection, then let it fall. This will never work.

After dressing and combing the tangles from my wet hair, I open the bathroom door to find Bryce leaning against the bed. My feet carry me forward until I'm pressed against him. My arms wrap around his waist as tears stream down my face.

"Hey," he whispers, "I've got you."

I pull away and force a tight smile. "Let's go out onto the deck."

"Okay," he says.

He holds my hand as we walk, gently rubbing his thumb across my knuckles in a soothing manner. When we reach the glass doors, Bryce releases me long enough to jog to the kitchen and grab two bottles of water. I don't move, following him with my eyes, drinking him in. This might be the last peaceful moment between us.

We walk to the rail and stare out at the ocean. Bryce's patience is unending. He doesn't say a word, letting me gather my thoughts. I take a water bottle from him and twist off the cap then take a long drink. Even though I was in the ocean less than an hour ago, the thirst is already building to an uncomfortable feeling. I guess I know why now.

"I thought about lying," I say, still staring at the frothy waves. "I could make something up, keep the truth from you forever."

"Kai-"

"I can't," I say, cutting him off. "I can't lie to you. I care about you too much." I look over at him for the first time, lifting one side of my mouth into a half grin. "Besides, you'd know if I was lying anyway."

"Yes," he replies, his face serious.

"I'm sorry. I shouldn't have even considered it. I'm just scared."

"Of what?"

I swallow thickly. "I'm scared that you'll push me away. That you won't...love me." My voice drops to a whisper with the last two words, and my eyes drop to my hands.

"Kai, look at me." When I meet his eyes, he continues, "That's never going to happen."

I sniff as my eyes start to burn again. "We'll see."

I take his hand and lead him to the circle of patio furniture in the corner. I take a seat on a bench and pull him down next to me. I try to release his hand, but he tightens his grip on mine and nods, encouraging me to speak.

When I say nothing, he asks, "Why was your mom out in the ocean, and where did she go?"

"Home," I say, then bark out a laugh. "Ms. Coraline wasn't lying. My mom really was home."

"Kai, you're not making any sense."

"I'm sorry," I say, sobering. I'm feeling slightly hysterical, and I don't know if I can get through this with the way my nerves are jumping under my skin. "Bryce," I start, remembering a conversation we once had, "can you do something for me?"

"Anything."

"Do you remember when I asked you if you were making me feel something? You said you weren't, but that you could. You said you would never do that to me unless I asked."

"I remember."

"Well, I'm asking. Can you cast a spell to make me calm? I feel like I'm going to explode with tension and I don't know if I can get through this conversation feeling this way."

He smiles, one of the real ones he reserves only for me. "I can fix that."

"Thank y-"

My words are cut off by his lips pressing against mine. I gasp in surprise, and he takes advantage of my open mouth to deepen the kiss. His tongue feels like silk against mine, and I can't help but fist my hands into his t-shirt, pulling him closer. Electricity pulses through my body, intensifying as Bryce pulls me over and guides my knees to either side of his hips.

As my hunger grows, my breathing becomes erratic, mimicking the bees now buzzing in my stomach. I've never felt this way before, but I like it. I lean forward on instinct, pressing my chest against his, the friction igniting me like lighter fluid on an already raging inferno. A growl emanates from Bryce's throat, pushing my desire even higher.

I'm lifted up for a brief second before I find myself lying on the cushioned bench. Bryce's lips never left mine, but our positions are now reversed, with him above me and our bodies flush from the chest down. The sudden flip shocks me out of the haze of desire, and I freeze, unsure of what is going to happen next.

Bryce's weight is gone in an instant. I sit up and watch him pace back and forth in front of me, raking his hands through his hair in agitation. I open my mouth to apologize, but he speaks before I can utter a syllable.

"Oh, God, Kai. I didn't mean for that to happen."

"Oh," is all I manage to choke out, his rejection causing my throat to close with emotion.

"No," he yells, taking his seat next to me and grabbing both my hands in a firm grip. "That's not what I meant."

"Okay," I say, unconvinced.

"I'm messing this up. I meant to say I'm sorry and that I didn't mean for it to go that far, right now. I was only trying to get you to relax. Without magic. It was a stupid idea."

My eyes widen and he shakes his head, releasing one of my hands to pinch the bridge of his nose. "Okay," he says, taking a deep breath, "let me start again. I thought I'd give you a kiss to calm you down. It was stupid because I should have known that if you kissed me back, I'd lose control. I want you too much and now is definitely not the time," he waves his arm around us, "or the place."

I can't fight the smile trying to form on my face. "I think I lost control first."

Bryce groans, closing his eyes, "Don't remind me or I'll be back on top of you before you can blink."

A short laugh escapes my mouth, and I stare at him. I'm sure awe is etched across my face. "You did it," I say. "I'm completely relaxed, no magic necessary."

He smiles at me for a brief moment before his face grows serious. "Okay, tell me everything."

***

"Say something."

Bryce's eyes are trained on the sea, scanning back and forth like he's trying to find proof of everything I just told him. The sound of my voice seems to break him from the trance. He turns toward me, pain etched on his face. Panic blooms in my chest. What if he doesn't believe me? What if he does but can't handle it? What if he pushes me away now that he knows the truth?

"How long do you have?"

"Huh?"

He grasps my shoulders in a firm grip, his eyes wild with fear. "How much longer will you be human?"

"I-I don't know."

My panic must break through the haze of his own because he loosens his grip and smooths out his expression. "Sorry," he says, pulling me into a tight hug. "I didn't mean to scare you. I just need to know how long I have to fix this. I can't lose you. I won't."

The tension in my body eases at his words. He's not going to push me away. He's going to stand beside me, helping me find a way out of this horrible situation. I wrap my arms around his waist and hug him back.

"Thank you."

He pulls away and takes my hand, leading me into the house. We head straight for the sofa and sit down. His knees brush against mine as we angle toward each other. Taking both of my hands in his, Bryce begins to speak.

"Kailani, I've been devoted to you since the first time we met and you caught me checking out your butt." He shoots me a cocky grin, then grows serious again. "I love you. Nothing is going to change that. I'm going to do everything I can to keep you here."

I nod, a constriction in my throat robbing me of my ability to speak. I swallow, trying to clear it. "Okay," is all I can manage to get out.

"I'm sure turning someone from one species to another is a heavy spell, one I'm not experienced enough to perform. That's if I could even find one." He increases the pressure on my hands. "My parents will be home in a week. Even sooner if I can manage to get a hold of them. They'll know what to do."

His conviction is reassuring, but I'm still scared. What if I don't have that long? What if I die from dehydration first? Or stay too long in the ocean and grow a tail? A shudder runs though me.

"What is it?" he asks.

"This is a lot for you to take on, Bryce. Are you sure it's worth it?"

He straightens his shoulders, causing his chest to puff out. "You're worth it."

A small tentative smile lifts my lips. "I love you."

That is the first time I've said it out loud. It feels good to put my feelings into words. Bryce's reaction makes it feel even better. His eyes drift shut and a moan echoes from his chest.

"Say it again."

My smile widens. "I love you, Bryce Howell."

A split second later I'm on my back with Bryce hovering over me, his lips devouring mine. Before I can manage to get my arms around his neck, he's gone, and I'm being pulled back up into my previous sitting position.

"Sorry," he says, panting.

I shake my head, trying to get my own breathing under control. "Don't apologize."

His white teeth flash just before he leans forward and places a gentle kiss on my lips. Pulling away slightly, he whispers, "To be continued," before pressing his lips against mine one more time.

Standing, he paces in front of me, his eyebrows drawn down. "Okay. So Coraline casts a spell to make your mother human for a favor...one she never collects, as far as we know." He looks at me for confirmation. I nod, and he continues pacing. "Then she makes you human, but her price is that your dad will be changed into a merman and your mother will be her slave."

"Yes, that's the gist of it."

"There's one thing I don't understand."

"Just one?"

Suppressed

He doesn't acknowledge my smart remark. "Why was keeping you away from me so important that she was willing to throw away everything and reverse the spell?"

"She's evil, and she wants me to be miserable?" I offer up.

Bryce stops his pacing and meets my eyes, shaking his head. "I don't think so. There are any number of less drastic things she could have done to keep us apart. She threw away everything because it was important. Very important. We have to figure this out, Kai. It could be the key to everything."

"I can ask my mom. If I see her again, that is."

"I'm sure she's out there, waiting for you to go back into the ocean."

"I'm kind of scared, Bryce. I almost didn't make it out in time today."

He takes my hand and pulls me up from the couch. Wrapping his arms around me, he squeezes. "I know you're scared, but you have to go back. You know the headache is going to come back. The thirst, the fatigue...it all has to be connected. You'll just have to be more careful and only stay out a few minutes at a time."

"You're right." I tighten my grip on his waist then back out of his arms. "I'll go back out tomorrow." I lift one eyebrow. "But right now, I need something from you."

"Oh, yeah?" he says, taking a few stalking steps forward as I back up.

"Yeah," I say, laughing as he catches me. He lifts me off my feet and twirls me around.

He stops spinning, letting my feet find purchase beneath me. He trails kisses up my neck to my ear. My eyes drift shut as I exhale roughly.

"What do you need?" he whispers, a suggestive note to his voice.

I pull back so I can look into his eyes. Keeping the eye contact, I move my face toward his, unhurried. Just before our lips touch, I freeze.

"Food," I whisper, before jerking away and running toward the kitchen.

"Oh, I'm going to get you for that!" Bryce yells.

I run around the center island and stop, my breath heaving and my eyes locked on the door.

Suppressed

When Bryce doesn't run in after me, a pang of disappointment streaks through me. I shrug and turn, intending to head to the sink for a drink.

I bump into a solid wall of chest and arms tighten around me before I can even think about escaping. "Gotcha," Bryce says, tickling my sides. "Resurgo."

"No fair," I whine. "You used magic."

He chuckles, releasing me and heading toward the fridge. "All's fair in love and war, right?"

I grin, shaking my head. Walking to the sink, I fill a glass with water and chug it down. Turning, I brace a hip against the counter and watch Bryce as he makes two turkey and cheese sandwiches. He's humming a song I've never heard, his deep voice vibrating from his chest.

He catches me watching and smiles. That's when I know. We *will* figure this out. I refuse to let anyone or anything tear me away from him. We belong together.

His smile grows, teeth flashing against tan skin. He can feel my conviction. My refusal to be beaten. My love. I nod, reaffirming the emotions he sensed from me.

"I feel the same way," he says, walking over to the table with a plate in each hand. "Now, let's eat."

Chapter 22

"Are you guys sleeping in the same bed?"

The bite of pizza I was in the process of swallowing lodges in my throat and threatens to go down my windpipe. Coughing, I grab my water and wash it down. Tears trail from my eyes as I breath in and out, trying to regain my composure.

Ana laughs. "Sorry. Bad timing."

It's almost too cold to sit outside, but I wanted some privacy to talk to her. When I saw her in the lunch line, I led her out to the table in the courtyard. I look over at her huddled next me, the wind blowing her hair across her face. I've been trying to come up with a way to tell her about my conversation with my mom, so her question threw me for a loop.

"Well? Are you going to answer me?"

I can't help but grin. "Yes."

"Oooh," she sing-songs, "boom-chicka-bow-wow."

"Shut up. It's not like that. Bryce is a perfect gentleman. He just doesn't want me to be alone. I have been having trouble sleeping." My grin fades.

Ana sobers. "Sorry, Kai. I know you've been going through a lot."

"You have no idea."

She cocks an eyebrow at me. "What does that mean?"

I glance around to make sure we're still alone. No one else is outside in this weather, so I decide that now is as good a time as any. I angle my body toward hers and lean closer. The grave look on my face lets Ana know I'm serious, and she drops her sandwich and crosses her arms over her chest.

"I saw my mom yesterday."

"What? Where?"

I take a deep breath and exhale slowly. "While I was swimming." Her mouth opens to speak, but I cut her off. "Just let me get this all out, okay?"

"Okay," she says, mimicking zipping her mouth shut and throwing an imaginary key over her shoulder.

"She popped up out of nowhere and

explained...everything to me. Why she left, where she's been, what we are.

"You promised!" I exclaim when her mouth opens again. "So..." I trail off, taking another deep breath. "We're mermaids."

I stare into her eyes as I wait for her reaction. I see confusion, disbelief, wonder, then acceptance cross her features. "Okay," she says, drawing the word out.

"I know this is hard to believe. I mean, even harder than believing Bryce is a witch. I can't exactly prove it to you."

"Kai, I trust you."

"Thank you." My eyes start burn with unshed tears as I tell her everything. "That's why she ran out."

"What about you? Why are you still here?"

"I don't know the biology of it, but my change is more gradual. I think it has to do with me being half human. I've been feeling symptoms of severe dehydration and only getting in the ocean makes me better. But if I stay out too long, I'll grow a tail and be stuck that way forever."

"But, if you could be with your mom and dad..." she lets the suggestion trail off, a frown marring her face.

I shake my head. "I can't. My mom said that merpeople marrying humans is frowned upon, children between them is forbidden. I'm an abomination. They would kill me. That's why my dad sacrificed himself to keep me human."

"An abomination? That seems harsh."

"That's what my mom told me. I don't really understand it. She made me swear that if I felt my legs tingling I would leave the water immediately. It's a sign that the change is starting."

Ana stares at the ground for several beats, her eyes wide and unfocused. I remain quiet, letting her absorb everything I told her. My leg bounces beneath the table, an outlet for my nervous energy. Finally, she looks back at me.

"Okay. What do we do now?"

I release the breath I've been holding. "Bryce is trying to get in touch with his parents. They may be able to recreate the spell that Ms. Coraline used to make me and Mom human."

Suppressed

Ana nods but remains silent. I don't know how I got so lucky to have such amazing people in my life. I told her I'm a mermaid, and she barely batted an eye. I reach over and squeeze her hand.

"Thank you."

"For what?"

"For being such a good friend. For understanding and not freaking out. For being you."

Smiling, she says, "I'm your best friend. Always have been. Always will be. Nothing is going to change that, even if you *are* a fish."

"Oh, my God, shut up!" I shove her as she breaks out into giggles. "I am going back out today after school," I say, growing serious.

"Isn't that dangerous? I mean, aren't your mother's people after you?"

"I don't think so. My mom made it sound like I would only be in danger if I completely turn and get stuck out there."

"But why risk it? Can't you go more than a day without getting too sick? You look okay right now."

"Yeah. I could wait. But I need to try to find my mom again. I have to ask her something."

"What?"

I lean closer as a group of kids leaving the cafeteria hurry by. "Don't you think it's strange that Ms. Coraline was so determined to keep me way from Bryce? She gave up everything when she broke that spell. We all know she's a witch now. We could tell people and the rumors, even if no one believes them, would hurt her reputation. She gave up her house servants. She gave up the favor my mom still owed her from the very beginning. For what? To make me unhappy? There has to be more to it, and I'm betting my mom knows the reason."

"Hello, ladies."

Ana and I both look up to see Bryce sitting down across from us. He smiles at Ana, one of the real ones he usually reserves for me. It warms my heart to see it even when it's not directed at me. He looks at me and winks.

"I just finished telling Ana everything," I say.

"I figured," he says, glancing at her quickly before those blue eyes settle on me again. "I could feel your anxiety fade away from inside the building."

Suppressed

"Okay, lovebirds," Ana says, standing up. "I'm coming over after school. I want to be there if Kai does speak to her mom."

"Thanks, Ana," I say.

"Always," she says, reading the extra meaning in my words.

I watch her walk away until she disappears through the door leading into the building. My eyes turn to Bryce, who's staring at me, a soft smile curving his lips.

"What?" I ask.

"She really is a good friend, isn't she?"

"The best."

Wendi L. Wilson

Chapter 23

I jerk with a start at the sound of the bell ringing. Last period is over, and I've been lost in my own head the entire class. I jot down the homework listed on the blackboard, hoping I didn't miss anything too important. The book we're reading for class is one I've already read three times, so I should be okay.

Gathering my belongings and shoving them into my backpack, I look up and realize I'm the only person left in the room. Even our professor is gone. Everyone is always in a rush to get out of here on Friday afternoon, and today is no exception.

As I near the door, someone steps in and blocks my way out. The stench of musky perfume hits me before I can get a look at the person's face. Taking a quick step back so we don't collide, I suppress a groan when I see who it is. Lanie Thompson.

She stares at me without speaking, her nose scrunched up like the mere sight of me offends her. I don't have time for this. My mother could be waiting for me, even now.

"What do you want, Lanie?" I ask, my irritation clear.

"Oooh, look who has claws after all." She takes a step forward, invading my personal space. I try to hold my breath. Her perfume really is gag-worthy. "Mine are sharper than yours, trust me."

I want to step away, if for no other reason than to breathe clean air, but I know she'll take it as a sign of weakness. I have to stand my ground. I stare at her expectantly, hoping she'll make her point quick and get out of my way.

"I thought I made it pretty clear," she says, her voice turning conversational, "that Bryce Howell is mine."

I bite my tongue to keep from laughing in her face. I'm pretty sure she wouldn't hesitate to claw my eyes out if I did that. I take second to school my features before responding.

"Does he know that?" I ask, my voice syrupy-sweet.

Her nostrils flare with anger. "I don't know what kind of spell you're weaving around him." I make a choking sound at the word "spell." She narrows her eyes. "What did the old lady do after I told her you were seeing him?"

"What?" I ask, my voice deepening with a flare of anger.

She smiles, finally getting a reaction out of me. "Oh, didn't she tell you? My mother and I ran into her at dinner last Thursday night. I just had to ask her what she thought about you hanging out with the new kid." She bats her eyelashes and lightens her voice. "He's kind of a bad boy, you know. Flirting with all the girls. Kai should be careful or he'll break her heart."

My backpack drops to the floor. Balling my hands into fists, I scowl at her. I don't know if I've ever been this angry. She ends her reenactment of her conversation with Ms. Coraline and shoots me a nasty smile. Her self-satisfaction is clear.

"Do you know what you've done?" I ask, stepping even closer.

Rage takes over, clouding my vision and stiffening my entire body. This stupid girl destroyed my life, and she doesn't even know it. I could kill her right now. At the very least, rip her hair out. My arm snakes out of its own volition, and a loud crack echoes through the room as my hand connects with her cheek.

A look of disbelief crosses her face. Her hand covers the red mark I left. The slap didn't relieve any of my anger. My face is hot and my hands are trembling. I take another step forward as she steps back.

"You stupid..."

I trail off as someone appears in the doorway behind her. Breathing hard, Bryce leans against the doorjamb, looking from me to Lanie and back again. My anger recedes as I register the worry on his face. He must have felt it from the parking lot. I'd been projecting again.

"Is there a problem here?" he asks.

Lanie pushes her way past him without a word, her hand still pressed against her cheek. The sound of her heels clicking against the tile fades in time with the last of my anger. The only thing left is regret.

"Did you hit her?" Bryce asks, stepping into the room and closing the door behind him. "I could feel your anger from outside. What happened?"

Suppressed

"It was her," I say, jumping forward into his arms. The aftermath of my rage is tears, and they pour freely down my face as I speak. "She told her."

"Told who, what?"

I pull my face away from his now wet shirt to look into his eyes. They're filled with concern. "Ms. Coraline. She told her we were hanging out together the night before everything happened. It's all Lanie's fault. Just because she wants you for herself."

Bryce pulls me back into his chest as fresh tears stream from my eyes. "It's okay," he whispers, kissing the top of my head. "We are going to fix this, Kai. I promise. Everything will be okay."

I pull away, sniffing loudly. "Can you fix it if I kill Lanie Thompson?"

He barks out a laugh and slings is arm over my shoulders. Grabbing my backpack with his free hand, he slings it over his shoulder and opens the door. Leading me out into the hallway, he leans over, bringing his mouth close to my ear.

"How about if I cast a spell to grow warts all over her face?"

"You can do that?" I ask, excitement coursing through me.

He laughs. "You've got a dark, catty side, Kailani Ericson."

We step out into the bright, afternoon sunshine. The parking lot is mostly empty. I see Lanie Thompson's car squealing tires as she speeds from the lot. Good. She better run. Ana's car pulls up beside us, windows rolled down.

"Get in," she calls out over the blaring music.

Bryce opens the door of her electric blue coupe and climbs into the backseat, leaving shotgun to me. Once we're settled, Ana turns down the music and pulls out of the parking lot.

"I'm sleeping over tonight," she says.

"You are?"

She looks into her rearview mirror at Bryce. "If it's okay with you, that is."

"It's fine with me," Bryce says, smiling.

I slump back into my seat and stare through the windshield. Ana and I have never had a sleepover before. Ms. Coraline would never allow it. I glance over at Ana with one eyebrow raised.

Suppressed

"What did you tell your mom?"

"That I'm staying at your house."

"She didn't think that was weird? I've never been allowed to have a sleepover before."

Ana winks at me. "I told her the old hag is out of town and your mom said I could."

"Do you think she'll call to talk to my mom?"

"No. She trusts me." Her face darkens slightly with guilt. "Anyway," she says, brushing it off, "she'll call my cell, if anything. We'll just tell her your mom ran out for pizza or something."

"Okay, if you're sure."

"I am."

I smile at her. "Thanks, Ana." I stare at the trees along the driveway, then a thought hits me. "You know, technically, you're not lying. This really is my house. Sort of."

Ana pulls the car to stop in front of the garage. With a skeptical look, she asks, "Is it a 'what's his is yours' kind of thing?"

I laugh. "No, nothing like that. This was my home when I was born. Old man McCormick was my great-grandfather."

"What? I never knew that!"

I shrug. "I didn't either. My mom told me yesterday. I wish I could have met him, but Ms. Coraline never allowed it."

We climb out of the car and head inside. Walking to the kitchen for some water, I tell Ana what happened with Lanie after school. I only get as far as her confession when Ana breaks in. Hands on hips, she all but growls, "She did what?"

"She told Ms. Coraline I was seeing Bryce. She made it sound like he's a bad boy-"

"I am pretty bad ass," Bryce interjects, reaching past me to grab a cup from the cabinet.

"-like that would make the old hag force me to stop seeing him," I continue without acknowledging Bryce's interruption. "She had no idea I'd already been ordered to stay away from him. Regardless, her petty, jealous actions lost me my home, my mother, and possibly my humanity."

Ana snarls under her breath. "What did you do?"

My face heats with a blush. Bryce laughs and throws an arm over my shoulders. "She slapped her." A dreamy look crosses his face as he glances up at the ceiling. "I wish I could have seen it."

"You weren't with her?"

He shakes his head, releasing me. "No. I got there right after. I was waiting in the parking lot when I felt Kai's anger. I ran but didn't make it in time to see Lanie Thompson get what's been coming to her." He heaves an overly-dramatic, disappointed sigh.

"What do you mean, you felt her anger?"

"Oh... I, uh, guess we left that out when we told her everything," Bryce says, looking at me.

"Bryce can feel people's emotions," I explain. "It's one of his many gifts." I smile at him. "We don't know why, but my emotions come through stronger. And, if I concentrate, I can actually project my thoughts to him."

"Seriously?"

"Seriously."

"That's cool," she says.

"Yeah. It is."

I finish off my water and set my glass in the sink. I can feel a headache coming on. I just went swimming yesterday. It shouldn't be happening this soon. It feels like a ticking time bomb waiting to go off. How much longer before I'll feel sick as soon as I leave the water?

"I'm going to go change into my bathing suit," I say, trying to escape the kitchen before Bryce feels my pain.

"Hey," he says softly, catching my wrist as I try to brush by him. "You okay?"

I should have known I couldn't hide anything from him. "Yeah. At least I will be when I talk to my mom."

He pulls my hand to his mouth and kisses my knuckles. Ana makes a gagging noise and I laugh, pulling my hand from his.

"I'll be right back," I say over my shoulder as I leave the room.

I jog up the stairs to Bryce's room. My feet carry me to the nightstand, and I pick up my mother's locket. I run my fingers over the inscription. I think about my parents, trapped in an underwater world

Suppressed

where my father is a prisoner. I guess the monsters are literal, after all.

Wendi L. Wilson

Chapter 24

"Mom?"

My feet kick at the cold water while I spin in circles. I've been calling out for my mother for several minutes, but she hasn't appeared. I dive under and swim a little further out. I can't go too far. I have to be able to reach shore fast when the tingling starts.

"Merryn!"

I yell her name as loud as I can, hoping...I don't know what I'm hoping. She's not here. I turn back toward the shoreline and doggy-paddle. Taking my time, I call out to her again and again, expecting her pop up at any moment.

A shiver runs down my spine, not from the cold temperature. Panic seizes me. I freeze and dip under the water. I open my eyes and see two legs. Relief floods me. I am not changing. I shoot back to the surface and tread water once more.

A tingling starts in my toes. I need to get out of the water. Now. I swim forward, thinking about the strange shiver I felt. A flash of light catches my attention, and I stop swimming, treading water once more. I see it again.

The flash comes from Ms. Coraline's deck. I squint and can make out her large form leaning against the railing, a pair of binoculars pressed against her eyes. She's watching me. She probably heard me calling for my mother. She probably knows I know the truth. She is probably enjoying this.

The tingling in my toes moves up my feet into my ankles so I strike out for shore again. Swimming at top speed, I make it in less than a minute. Ana and Bryce are waiting for me with a towel stretched between them. As soon as my feet hit dry sand, they wrap it around me and mutter consoling words about me not finding my mom.

I glace back over at Ms. Coraline, who's still standing on her deck, watching me. The binoculars hang from a chain around her neck. Ana and Bryce's eyes follow mine until they catch sight of her too. Ana gasps, and a snarl vibrates from Bryce's chest.

They hustle me toward Bryce's house, each with an arm around me from either side. A loud cackle erupts from behind us, but we don't acknowledge it. By silent agreement, we keep moving and ignore the old hag's obvious pleasure. We refuse to give her the satisfaction.

"Tell her," Ana says as we ascend the steps from the beach.

"Tell me what?" I ask, turning my attention to Bryce.

"My parents called while you were swimming. They're coming home on Sunday."

Panic blooms in my chest, and my feet skid to a halt when we reach the top. Bryce's parents. I've never met them. It would be nerve racking enough if I was just a normal girlfriend. I'm anything but. What if they refuse to help me? What if they kick me out?

"Hey," Bryce says, tightening his hold on me. "Breathe. They are going to help us."

"They are?"

He smiles. "Yes. They are."

"What did they say? Do they know a spell to make me human?"

The corners of Bryce's mouth turn down. "No. Not yet. But they are in the midst of some of the best witches in the country. My dad said they would ask around, discreetly, and see if anyone in the coven has any ideas."

"Okay." The word sounds hopeless, even to my own ears.

"Hey," Ana says, draping an arm across my shoulders, "don't worry. I have always had your back, always will. Now you have Bryce and his parents too. We *will* fix this."

"You're right," I say, wrapping my arm around her waist and squeezing. Releasing her and taking a step back, I kiss Bryce on the cheek. "I'm going to go take a shower and change."

Bryce nods and looks at Ana. "Want to help me make dinner?"

I smile at Ana's groan and noncommittal answer as I trudge up the stairs. She'll try to find a way to make it look like she's helping while Bryce does all the work. A soft snicker rattles in my chest. Bryce will pick up on her scheming, of that I have no doubt.

After my shower, I dig a pair of jeans and a t-shirt from my bag. All of my clothes are still in there because I don't know how long I'll be here. After dressing, I sit on the edge of the bed.

Suppressed

My watch and my mother's necklace still rest on the night stand. I stare at them for several seconds before making a decision. I pick up the watch and strap it to my wrist. It feels good, like a part of me was missing while it sat collecting dust for the last few days.

Grabbing the locket, I open it and stare at the picture of my father. He was so handsome. Is. He *is* so handsome. I swipe my eyes to clear my vision. If Bryce's parents help me, I will never meet my dad. If they don't, I may join him in his prison. Or worse.

Rolling my shoulders and wagging my head, I attempt to shake off my dejection. I clasp the chain around my neck and drop the locket underneath my shirt. The cool metal causes a shiver to run down my spine. I press against it through my shirt until it warms. Leaving the room, I finger comb the tangles from my wet hair as I head down the stairs.

Laughter draws me to the kitchen. I stand in the doorway unnoticed and watch Ana rush around the table and stop on the other side, breathing hard. A squeal erupts from her as she jumps and runs back to the other side of the kitchen. She yells my name when she spots me, then sprints over, pulling me into the room and hiding behind me.

"Help me," she whines in a high-pitched voice.

Before I can ask her what she's hiding from, electric tingles streak across my cheeks. Warm hands frame my face just before smooth lips brush across mine. I keep my eyes open, seeing nothing but an empty kitchen before me. Yet, the feeling of Bryce kissing me is undeniable. This is so weird.

"Resurgo."

I resist the urge to jump back when he appears, his face inches from mine. He's proud of himself, if his bright smile is any indication. I can't help but smile back.

"Well, that was weird," Ana says, bringing us back to reality.

Bryce laughs. "You haven't seen anything yet."

I open my mouth to comment on how awesome it is, to be able to share everything with Ana, to get rid of all the secrets, but the ringing of Bryce's phone cuts me off. He picks it up from the counter and looks at the screen, his face turning serious.

"It's my dad," he says, tapping the screen. "Hey, Dad."

He holds up one finger and mouths, "Be right back," before walking out of the kitchen and into the living room. I want to follow, to at least hear his side of the conversation, but Ana grabs my wrist and holds me where I am.

"Give him some privacy," she says. "I'm sure he'll tell us if it concerns you."

I slump my shoulders in defeat and nod. "Okay. You're right." I glance around the kitchen. "Why was Bryce chasing you around, anyway?" I ask, cocking one eyebrow at her.

"Oh, that? Well, I tried to get out of helping by pretending I didn't know how to chop lettuce. He grabbed the knife from me and started demonstrating. I guess I couldn't hide my amusement, because he looked at me and accused me of lying. When playing innocent didn't work, I ran away." She laughs. "He muttered something and suddenly I couldn't see or hear him."

"Yeah, he does that a lot," I say, chuckling.

"I froze, listening for any hint of where he might be, then I felt fingers tugging on my hair. I screamed and ran. That's when you came in and rescued me." She bats her eyelashes at me.

"Hey," Bryce says from the doorway. I don't like the look on his face.

"What is it?"

"My parents found something," he says. "It's Ms. Coraline. I think I know why she is so determined to keep us apart."

Chapter 25

My back is straight, and my knee bobs up and down as I wait, unable to relax on the plush sofa. Bryce told me to come in here and wait while he makes us some coffee. Ana sits next to me, any attempt to finish making dinner forgotten in the wake of Bryce's announcement. I don't think I could eat anyway. My stomach is tied in knots.

Ana puts her hand on my knee, exerting pressure to stop the bouncing. "Relax," she murmurs. "This is a good thing, right? We need all the information we can get."

I blow out the breath I've been holding and slump back. "Right," I say, not sounding totally convinced, even to my own ears.

Bryce walks in carrying a tray with three steaming mugs, and I sit up, my back stiff once more. I bite my lip to keep from screaming at him to tell me what his dad said. I know he'll tell me everything. I just need to be patient. That's easier said than done.

"Well?" I demand a few seconds later.

Bryce's lips turn up, but the smile doesn't quite reach his eyes. He raises the coffee mug to his lips, blowing the liquid for a moment before taking a sip. He doesn't break eye contact with me. The room is silent but for the soft clink of his mug hitting the glass table.

"Okay," he says, turning his eyes from me to Ana, then back again. "First of all, my parents found a spell they think may work to keep you human."

"They did?"

I roll my shoulders to ease the tension and relax my posture. Bryce's parents may be able to fix me. My body feels lighter, like an enormous weight has been lifted. I'm going to be okay. I try to smile, but it drops as soon as it starts to form.

"Tell me about Ms. Coraline."

The pressure of Ana's hand on my knee increases, an attempt to comfort me. Bryce takes a fortifying breath and lets it out slowly. He picks up his coffee and takes another sip. He's stalling.

"Bryce."

"Okay," he says, his voice defensive. "I'll tell you."

Suppressed

"Thank you." I soften my voice, an apology for my waspish tone.

"There are certain people... witches, called diviners."

"Diviners?"

"Yes. Kind of like how I have the ability to feel emotions, they have an ability too. Diviners have visions." His lips take on a whitish hue as he presses them together. "Visions of the future."

"Okay," I say. "That's cool, but what does have to do with Ms. Coraline?"

"One of these diviners had a vision about Ms. Coraline and Kai?" Anna says, her voice breathy.

A nerve ticks in Bryce's jaw. He's grinding his teeth together which scares me more than his words. "What is it Bryce? What did they see?"

"My mom and dad were asking around about a spell to help you," he says in a quiet voice. "Evelyn, the diviner in our coven overheard them say Ms. Coraline's name. She recognized it."

His voice trails off, and he takes a deep breath. Letting it out slowly, his dark blue eyes travel over my face. He's been standing for the whole conversation, but now he sits beside me opposite Ana and takes my hand in his. Small electric tingles race across my palm, causing me to shiver.

"Do you ever wonder why it feels like that every time we touch?"

"You feel it too?"

"Of course, I do."

"Huh. I thought it was just me."

"Um, what are you guys talking about?" Ana asks. I'd almost forgotten she was there.

"Well," I say, looking over at her, "every time we touch it feels charged, like static electricity. I always thought it was just my nerves."

"I never really thought much about it," Bryce says, "except that it felt amazing."

"Are you saying there is more to it?" I ask.

He nods. "Kai, we're synergetic."

The heat of Ana's body warms my arm as she leans in closer. "What does that mean?" she asks when I remain silent.

"It means Kai and I are connected," Bryce says without taking his eyes off me. "Physically, mentally and spiritually connected."

A prickling sensation on the back of my neck has me twitching in my seat. "That... that's crazy. Just because we feel electricity when we touch... Bryce, there's a hundred love songs about that. It doesn't mean anything."

"What about the banana?"

"You can sense emotions. You've admitted mine come through stronger."

"Kai, come on. Sending a direct thought about a specific object is a lot more than sending strong emotions. Besides, Evelyn saw it."

"What did she see?" My heart beats an erratic rhythm in my chest.

"She saw us. You and me. We were on the beach under the light of a full moon. Coraline appeared, and you said her name. That's why Evelyn recognized it. We joined hands, and as we did, fire sparked from my palm and struck Coraline in the chest. She screamed, then vanished."

"That's insane. Ana," I say, looking to her for support, "tell him it's crazy."

Ana looks from me to Bryce and back again. "No. I think I've heard of this. My abuela told me a story once. There was a man, a very bad man, who controlled her village with his money and power. The people lived in fear, until one day, he disappeared. No one knew where he went, and no one cared. They were free.

"But Abuelita told me she saw what happened. She was taking a walk one night near the man's house when she saw a man and a woman walking hand in hand down his front walk. She said his door flew open when they neared it even though their hands were still joined, and neither had touched it.

"She heard shouts from inside and snuck around the house to peek into the window. She said she'd never forget what she saw. The woman's hand was still grasping the man's, but her other hand was extended. Abuelita said lightning shot from the woman's palm, straight into the bad man's heart, and he vanished. Poof. Just like that. I always thought it was a fairy tale she made up to help me to sleep."

"They must have been witches," Bryce says. "Or, at least the woman was. According to the elders, only a witch can have a truly synergetic connection to another person, be it a human, another witch, or... something else entirely."

He smiles at me, a smile full of warmth and affection to let me know that the 'something else entirely' part is just fine with him. I don't have it in me to smile back. This is too much. I can't. I just can't. My heart doubles the speed of its pounding, and the room starts to spin around me.

I reach out and grab Bryce's wrist. "Help."

The smile drops from his face, and he covers my hand with his, unlatching my grip. He wraps both hands around mine and mumbles something I can't quite make out over the buzzing sound in my ears. A warmth spreads from his hands into mine, up my arm and into my chest. My rigid spine relaxes inch by inch as the anxiety ebbs away, and my heart rate returns to normal.

"Thanks," I exhale. "I think I was having my first panic attack."

"All good?" he asks.

I nod. "So, we're synergetic. Connected. But, what exactly does that mean for us, and how did it happen?"

"It's kind of the stuff of legends," Bryce says, staring at our joined hands. He lifts his eyes to mine. "A bedtime story witches tell their young children, like a fairy tale. Every witch's soul has a twin out in the world somewhere. A perfect match in every way. The magic inside us reacts to the proximity of our twin... it enhances, passing back and forth from one to the other, until the two are connected by the magic."

"Are you saying we're *soulmates*?" I say, unable to stop the edge of derision in my voice.

Bryce smiles, ignoring my cutting tone. "Something like that."

"That's so romantic," Ana sighs, her voice overly dramatic.

"Shut up," I say out of the side of my mouth.

"Kai," Bryce says, and my attention snaps back to him. "I know this is a lot. I grew up on this story. You didn't. But think about it. The electricity between us, the strong emotional connection, the thought transfer... it all fits." His stare snags mine, making my eyes burn with emotion. "There's no one else I'd rather be connected with. It's you and me, Kai. Always."

Suppressed

I rub my eyes until the stinging subsides. "So, we are going to take down Ms. Coraline?" The corners of my mouth turn up at the thought.

"That's what the diviner saw." He pauses, and the pressure of his hands on mine increases. "I think Coraline has access to her own diviner. What if, at some point, her diviner had a vision about you and I vanquishing her? It would explain why she was so adamant from the very beginning that we have no contact. She thought she could control the situation by keeping us apart. When that didn't work, she reversed her spell. If you're a mermaid, we can't be together. We can't stand against her. We can't defeat her."

That makes sense. I can't believe I'm even thinking that. Witches, mermaids, spells, visions, soulmates... it's almost too much. Two months ago, I was just a normal girl, a maid's daughter, living a normal life. Now, I'm on the verge of growing a tail and leaving my witch boyfriend behind, exiled to the sea where angry, human-hating merpeople want to kill me for being half human. It's surreal.

My eyelids drift down, and I take a deep breath. Bryce's parents will be here tomorrow. They'll cast the spell, and I won't have to worry about becoming a mermaid. My mom's face flashes in my mind, but I push it away. One problem at a time. First, we need Bryce's parents to cast the spell to make me human. Then we can find my mom and deal with Ms. Coraline. I open my eyes and steel my spine.

"The old hag is going down."

Chapter 26

"Mom!"

I've only been in the water for a few minutes and already I feel a tingling sensation in my toes. I need to get out. Sucking a large gulp of air into my lungs, I dive under and swim toward the beach. By the time I get to water shallow enough to stand, the prickling has reached my knees.

Bryce is waiting for me on the sand, a fluffy towel stretched between his hands. I step closer, and he wraps it around me, pulling the ends tight.

"Everything okay?"

"It's happening faster and faster every time I go in. How long was I out there? Five minutes?"

"Something like that," he says. "No sign of your mom?"

I shake my head. "Bryce, I'm getting worried. What if something has happened? She said she'd be back. Where is she?"

"Hey," he says wrapping his arms around me and pulling me against his chest, "try not to worry. Your mom is tough. She'll be okay."

I step out of his arms and take his hand in mine. Silent, we stroll down the beach, ambling in the general direction of Bryce's house. I shiver as the cool air kisses my wet skin. Everything that happened from Bryce's phone call last night to Ana leaving this morning replays through my mind. The spell his parents found to make me human again. Synergetic soul twins. Prophetic visions. Bryce quietly stating he'd sleep in his parents' room so I could have my first real slumber party. Ana and I whispering until we both fell asleep. The smell of bacon and coffee waking us up. The sight of Bryce in the kitchen, the early morning light shining in his hair as he flipped pancakes onto plates for us.

When I headed into the water a few minutes ago, I had the strange feeling of being watched. I look over my shoulder at Ms. Coraline's house. I see nothing, but that doesn't mean she's not there. She is a witch, after all.

"Bryce," I say pulling him from his own thoughts. "Why didn't Ms. Coraline just kill me? Or you? She had us both trapped in my room yet she only teleported you home and reversed the spell that made me human. Wouldn't killing one, or both, of us been a more effective solution to her problem?"

"I don't know," he says, leading me toward the steps up to his deck. "Maybe she didn't want to deal with the hassle of getting rid of the bodies."

"She's a witch. I'm sure she could make us disappear just like that," I say, snapping my fingers. "There has to be something else."

Then it hits me. I remember her cackling laughter yesterday after I searched the waves for my mother and found nothing. The way she always looked so smug, ordering us around and reprimanding us for every imagined trespass. The tiny black kitten sailing through the air and landing in the sea.

"She wants us to suffer." I walk across the deck and plop down into a chair. "If I'm a mermaid and forced to live in the sea, we can't be together. I'm miserable, you're miserable. We can't use our synergy to defeat her. It's a win-win for Ms. Coraline with the added bonus that I'd probably be dead within a few days, killed by my own kind."

Bryce pulls me up and takes my seat, pulling me down into his lap. "Well, thanks to my parents, that's not going to happen."

"You're getting all wet," I say trying to wriggle free as his arms tighten around me.

"It's totally worth it."

I freeze at his tone and the insinuation in his voice. Realizing I had been practically rubbing my butt into his lap in my bid for freedom, my face heats up with what I know must be the brightest, rosiest blush in the history of all blushes. There's an apology on the tip of my tongue, but before I can utter it, I get a look at the smug, self-satisfied smile on his lips.

"Ugh. Jerk," I say, relaxing back against him.

His chuckle resonates through me before I feel his breath against my ear. "But teasing you is so much fun," he says before letting his lips brush against my cheek.

I push myself up, and this time Bryce releases me. "I'm going to go take a shower," I say.

"Okay," he says dejectedly, giving me sad, puppy dog eyes.

Suppressed

I lean over and press my lips against his. I quickly pull away, sidestepping his outstretched arms and his attempt to pull me back down into his lap. I run through the open doors before he can stand up, letting my laughter trail behind me.

I skip the stairs two at a time, feeling more lighthearted than I have in days. Bryce is right. His parents will be here tomorrow, they'll cast the spell to make me human, then Bryce and I can be together. I'll worry about Ms. Coraline later.

I rummage through my bag and pull out some warm clothes. I walk to the bathroom, closing the door behind me. My fingers freeze on the lockless knob. Will Bryce try to sneak in? Shaking my head at the ludicrous thought, I strip out of my wet bathing suit. I turn the shower to hot and run a brush through my hair as I wait for it to heat up.

Stepping into the humid spray, a sigh escapes my lips. It feels so good, warming the chill that has taken up residence in my bones. The scent of lavender hits my nose, and I smile. As much as I love the way Bryce smells, it's nice to have my own shampoo. I don't think his scent suits me, anyway.

I rinse the shampoo out and massage in some conditioner. Letting it sit, I lather up some soap on a washcloth and rub it up and down my arm. I close my eyes, imagining what it would feel like if Bryce were in here with me. If it were his hands slicking soap across my body. I feel my face heat with embarrassment at the thought, yet I can't stop the fantasy. I imagine him pulling me close, licking the water from my skin as the jets pound against us. His mouth finding mine, his hands roaming, his naked body molding against mine.

I grab the knob and turn it to the right until the water is freezing cold. Making short work of the rest of my shower, I turn off the water and step out. The towel feels soft and warm against my skin as I dry off as fast as possible, trying to block out the memory of my fantasy.

After dressing, brushing my teeth and towel-drying my hair, I hang my swimsuit over the shower doors to dry and leave the room. My face is blank and unemotional by the time I reach the bottom of the staircase. I wander through the house, looking for Bryce, finally finding him in the kitchen.

"Want some water?" he asks. His back is to me and he doesn't turn to look at me when he asks the question.

Suppressed

"Sure," I say.

He turns on the tap and fills a glass. I see his shoulders lift and sag back down before he turns to look at me. Color is riding high on his cheeks, and a fire is burning in his eyes as he walks toward me, his pace slow and measured.

"What?" I ask. He's acting weird.

"Nothing," he says, stopping a couple of feet away from me and stretching out his arm.

I take the glass and press it against my mouth, taking a sip before setting it on the table. Bryce's eyes are glued to my lips, and I see his nostrils flare as my tongue flicks out to lick them. He takes a small step forward before jerking back to where he was.

"Bryce, what's wrong?"

He shakes his head, as if to clear it, and sags down into one of the chairs at the table. I take the seat next to him and lean in, only to have him scoot his chair a few inches away. I straighten, my face heating with embarrassment and tears threatening to form in my eyes. I start to rise, intent on leaving, but Bryce's hand on my arm stops me.

"Wait. Kai, I'm sorry. Don't leave."

"It's okay…" My words trail off as I stare down at my lap.

"Kailani, look at me." When I raise my eyes to his, the tears spill over, and he swears. "Christ, Kai, please don't cry. I can't take it."

I sniff and scrub my face. "Sorry."

"No, please don't apologize. It's my fault. I…"

I wait several beats, but he doesn't finish his sentence. "You what?"

He inhales deeply and looks down at his hands, sighing. "I don't want to embarrass you, but whatever you're thinking is probably way worse." He takes another deep breath and a rush of words pours out on the exhale. "Our-mind-bond-is-getting-stronger-and-I-could-see-your-thoughts-from-the-shower."

"What?!"

The chair legs screech across the floor behind me as I jump to my feet. I feel sick. I might throw up any second, all over Bryce. Then my humiliation will be complete. I turn to leave, to rush from the room and dive into the ocean. Facing a hoard of angry, human-hating mermaids seems preferable to being here, facing Bryce. Before I can take a step, his hand snakes out and captures mine.

"Kai, please, don't leave. We should talk about this."

I lift my face toward the ceiling, my eyelids fused together. "Can we please not?"

His grip on my wrist is unrelenting. With a sigh, I reach back with my other hand and pull my chair forward before slumping into it. I can't look at him. I don't know if I'll ever be able to look at him again. He releases me, and I can see him lean forward from the corner of my eye.

"Kai. Look at me, please." I hear a sigh as I shake my head, never letting my gaze leave the table. "We don't have to talk about *what* you were thinking, but I think we should discuss the fact that I could see and hear it. You obviously weren't projecting on purpose."

"Obviously," I murmur.

He stays quiet for a moment. I wonder what he's thinking. I sneak a quick peek at him from beneath my eyelashes. He's staring at the floor, but his eyes raise to snag mine before I can look away.

"Maybe," he says, his tone soft and light as if he's cajoling a skittish animal, "your mind is more, I don't know... open when your emotions are heightened."

I snort out a self-deprecating laugh at his choice of words. Heightened emotions, indeed. He might as well call a duck a duck. I was hot and bothered. I've never had those kinds of thoughts about anyone before, and it's just my rotten luck that the first time I do, he gets front row seats to the show. Looking at him now, I remember the spark in his eyes when I first came downstairs.

Summoning up courage I didn't know existed, I ask, "Why did you pull away from me?"

Lifting a hand to his face, he scrubs it across his eyes and down to his chin. He leans in closer, propping his elbows on his knees. The fire reignites as his pupils dilate slightly, and a harsh breath expels from his nose. I sit, frozen, waiting for him to speak.

"Because what you were thinking, I've imagined at least a hundred times. After seeing it through your eyes, I wasn't sure I could control myself if you got too close."

Suppressed

"Oh," is all I can manage to say before his hands snap forward and grab mine.

He hauls me forward, up out of my seat and onto him so that I have no choice but to straddle his thighs. Not that I would have made another choice, had there been one. A need, stronger than I could have imagined possible surges through me. As soon as he releases my hands to wrap his around my hips, I thread my fingers through his hair and pull his head forward.

Bryce's kiss is possessive, yet his lips remain soft as they meet mine again and again. The hands on my hips drag me forward until my whole upper body is flush against his. He moans into my mouth, a mix of pleasure and pain that intensifies the heat building inside me. I squirm on his lap, not knowing what to do to ease the ache.

I can feel a shudder run through Bryce just before his mouth softens and his movements slow. He nibbles softly at my bottom lip before pulling back slightly to stare into my eyes. He lifts a hand to tuck a lock of red hair behind my ear.

"We should stop," he whispers, "before we go too far."

He must feel my body tense because he captures my lips again, kissing me softly until the tension flows out of me. He stands, pulling me up with him and wraps his arms around my waist. We hug, swaying back and forth for a few seconds before he pulls back to look at my face.

"Just so there's no misunderstanding, stopping that was the hardest thing I've ever done. When all of this is over, after my parents cast the spell to make you human again, after we've taken care of Ms. Coraline and found your mom, when we can just be two normal teenagers in love…"

"We'll pick up where we left off?" I ask when his words trail off.

His smile makes my toes curl. "Definitely."

Chapter 27

Bright, warm sunshine on my face is the first thing I notice as I wake. I blink my eyes a few times in an attempt to adjust to the light. Lifting my head, I glance at the window. We left the curtains open last night. The digits on the clock read 6:18 a.m. It's early.

I close my eyes, snuggling into the warmth of Bryce curled around me, his arm draped over my waist and his knees tucked up under mine. I can't stop the smile curving my lips as I think back to yesterday. We cuddled in his bed, watching television and snacking on junk food and soda. The conversation, the laughter, the kissing... That's what life is supposed to be like. That's what I've been missing all of mine, cooped up in that mausoleum with the old hag.

That thought spurs my brain into full function, the pistons firing one after another until I remember. Today is Sunday. Today is the day Bryce's parents come home.

"Bryce," I say, nudging him with my elbow. "Wake up."

"Humpf," is what his muttered response sounds like as he buries his head beneath the covers.

"Bryce."

I sit up and scoot over, then yank the covers off him. Whatever I was going to say flies right out of my head as I get a good look at him. His hair is standing up all over his head, and he has a slight stubble darkening his jaw. His bare chest curves and ripples as he stretches, and my mouth goes dry. He had on a shirt when I fell asleep last night.

"Bryce," I squeak out in a cracked voice. I clear my throat and try again. "Bryce." Great, now it sounds unnaturally deep. I close my eyes and groan. They fly back open when he laughs.

"Yes, Kailani?" he asks, lowering his voice to a deep timbre.

"Shut up," I say, swatting him on the chest. "I have a scratchy throat this morning."

All traces of humor flee is face, and he jumps from the bed. "You're dehydrated. I'll get you some water," he says, running from the room before I can say anything else.

I nod as he rushes from the room, realizing he's right. My mouth is as dry as a bone, and a throbbing pain in my temple beats in time with my heart. Closing my eyes against the pain, I flip the sheets back and swing my legs over the side of the bed. I massage my temples with two fingertips, hoping to alleviate some of the pain and crack my eyes open.

Air rushes into my lungs in an almost painful gasp as I get a good look at my legs. The skin is deathly white, dry, and cracked. It looks like the skin is peeling after a bad sunburn, with papery strips sticking out from my shins. I grasp the end of one and give it a tug. It peels up to my knee before coming loose and dangling from my fingertips.

A thud draws my attention to the doorway. Bryce is leaning against the door jamb in all his bare-chested glory, a glass of water in hand, his mouth hanging open. His eyes are glued to my legs. I grab the sheet and pull it over them, attempting to hide the grotesque shape they're in. Out of the corner of my eye I see Bryce shake himself and stand up straight.

"Here," he says, walking over and handing me the glass. "Drink it all."

I press the glass to my lips without a word and gulp it down, refusing to look at his face. I don't know why I'm so embarrassed. I just know I don't want him to see me this way. He is so perfect, and I have no idea why he would want to be with a freak like me.

"How long has it been since you last went swimming? Twelve hours?" he asks, pulling me from my dark thoughts.

I nod, raising my eyes to his. The concern I see in them causes the rhythm of my heart to stutter. I know he's said the words, told me how much he cares about me, but there's something about seeing the proof positive in his eyes that warms me in a way I've never felt before. Until Bryce.

"Let's go," he says, holding a hand out for me to take.

I place my hand in his and the warmth of his palm against mine shoots tingles up my arm. The sensation of the sheets brushing against my peeling legs sends shivers down my spine as he pulls me up from the bed. Something's not right. My knees buckle the second I try to stand. Lightning fast, Bryce catches me against his chest before I hit the floor.

Suppressed

Panic floods me as I stare up at him with wide eyes. "My legs don't work!"

Without a word, he loops his arm under my knees and picks me up, cradling me against his chest. I open my mouth to protest, but he shuts me down with a harsh look. I throw my arms around his neck as he bounds down the stairs, burying my face in his neck. The pain in my head intensifies with each step he takes.

Cool morning air caresses my skin as the scent of the sea invades my nose. The water calls to me, tempting me with its icy depths while at the same time frightening me. What if the change happens before I can get out? Last night it only took five minutes for the tingling to take over. What if the change is immediate? I'll be stuck. With murdering merpeople after me.

The sound of splashing pulls me from my thoughts, and I open my eyes, pulling my face away from Bryce's neck. He's wading out into the freezing water, taking me out to a depth where I can submerge.

"It's okay," I say, squirming for my release, "I can go from here."

His grip only tightens as he continues to wade out. "You can't walk, Kai. I've got you."

"But it's freezing." The whiny tone of my voice grates on my own ears.

His only response is a grunt as he trudges forward. When the water sloshes against my backside, he stops and releases my legs. Wrapping his now free arm around my back, he presses me against his chest. My legs float in the water, my feet not touching the bottom, as he stares into my eyes.

The pounding pain in my head recedes. The warmth of his chest seeps through my shirt and serves as a delicious contrast to the freezing water swirling around my legs. It's sexy as hell. All thoughts of mermaid tails and murder flee as his arms tighten around me. I want nothing more than to feel his lips against mine.

Kiss me. I muster all the feeling I can into the thought, mentally projecting it toward him. I feel more than hear the growl that parts his lips as they swoop down onto mine. He crushes his mouth against mine, and my hands tangle into his hair. I can feel his heart pounding against my chest, doubling in speed as our tongues meet.

Suppressed

Tingles shoot from my head down to my toes as he pours all of his love, his devotion and his worry for me into the kiss. I break away with a gasp, the emotions almost too much for me to handle. Without pausing a beat his lips lock onto my neck, sucking and kissing their way up to my ear.

"I love you," he says, his voice rough. "I want you." Then his mouth is back on my neck, his tongue lapping downward.

The tingling intensifies, centered in my lower abdomen with waves shooting down my legs. They seem to be working again, and with a mind of their own because they wrap around his waist with a tight grip. I hear Bryce groan, his lips suddenly ravaging mine again. Energy builds inside me, roaring to be expended.

A burning sensation in my feet brings me back to my senses like a gunshot. How long have we been out here? I don't know, but if the pain in my feet and the intensity of the tingling in my legs is any indication, it's been too long.

"Bryce," I say, ripping my lips from his.

The urgency of my voice must pierce the lust-fueled fog he was caught in because his eyes clear and his body tenses. Before I can utter another word, he turns and wades toward shore, me still wrapped around him like a spider monkey. As soon as his knees clear the water, he starts to jog and doesn't stop until we're up on his deck.

Lowering me to one of the chairs, he rushes inside and returns a few seconds later with a towel. I watch as he rubs it up and down first one leg, then the other, making sure the towel absorbs every drop. I stare at them in awe, the skin firm, pink and shiny, no trace of the strips of dead skin that were there before.

"Are you okay?" Bryce asks, wrapping the towel around my shoulders.

"I-I think s-so."

The cold air seeping is through my wet clothes, causing my teeth to chatter. I look up at Bryce, and his lips are tinged blue. He must have been freezing out there. The cold water may not affect me, but the same can't be said for him.

"Let's go," he says before I can open my mouth to apologize or thank him.

He pulls me from the chair and leads me inside, all the way upstairs and into the bathroom. I wait, my

Suppressed

arms holding the damp towel tightly around my shoulders as he turns on the tap and cranks the shower to the hottest setting. We wait in awkward silence for the water to heat up, neither of us attempting to make eye contact. When steam billows from the shower, he adjusts the temperature to a hot but comfortable level then turns toward me.

Pressing his lips against mine in one brief, hard kiss, he pulls back and says, "Hop in and warm up. I'll go take one in my parents' shower. Meet you downstairs?"

I nod, words still failing me, and he walks out, closing the door behind him with a gentle click. Dropping the towel, I rush into the hot spray, clothes and all. They're already wet, and I'm too cold to take the time to strip out of them.

Once the chills recede and life circulates back into my extremities, I strip down and toss the soggy clothes into the corner of the shower stall. Remembering what happened last time I took a shower, I think about a funny movie I saw once, going over the scenes in my head. I don't want my thoughts wandering back to what happened with

Bryce in the water. With my luck, I'd project my desire to him and embarrass myself again.

Once I'm clean and my hair is washed and conditioned, I turn off the water. Stepping out, I grab a fluffy towel and wrap it around my torso. Wrapping a second towel around my hair and twisting it into a turban, I open the door and peek my head out. Everything looks clear so I jet across the room, praying that won't come in.

I dress quickly, pulling a hoodie on over my t-shirt and jeans. After pulling on socks and shoes, I run my fingers through my wet hair and pull it up into a pony tail. I take a quick peek in the mirror. Not great, but it will have to do. I don't have the energy to put any more effort in.

I open the door and step out into the hall. Voices from downstairs meet my ears. Bryce must hear my footsteps because he calls my name as I reach the top of the stairs. I look down and see him waiting for me at the bottom with a sharp-dressed couple.

"Come on down, Kai. My parents are here."

Chapter 28

"So, you and my son are synergetic."

I nod, even though Mrs. Howell's words were a statement, not a question. I haven't spoken an actual complete sentence since I came downstairs and joined them in the living room. I don't know which makes me more nervous, the fact that they are Bryce's parents, that they're witches, or that Mrs. Howell won't stop staring at my hair. God, why didn't I take more time and do something with it? I knew they were coming today. She's probably decided I'm way too much of a slob to be her son's girlfriend, much less his fated, soulmate twin. That is, if she can even get past the whole mermaid thing.

"Mom," Bryce says, his hand on my knee tightening its grip, "stop staring. You're making her nervous."

Her eyes snap from me, to Bryce, and back again before her face softens. "I'm sorry for staring, Kailani. I've just never seen such a beautiful shade of red hair before."

"Thank you. It's the same as my mother's."

"Well, it's gorgeous."

"Ahem," Bryce's dad says, drawing everyone's attention. "What do you say we get to the matter at hand? We found a spell that may help you, Kailani, though it's not exactly the same as the original."

"What do you mean, Mr. Howell?"

"Please, call me Bran."

"Yes, and you may call me Celine."

"Thank you," I say nodding to each of them. "You were saying, Mr. How…uh…Bran?"

He lips turn up, and I feel instantly at ease. He and Bryce have the same smile. "Yes," he says, "as I was saying, the spell is different, but Celine and I think it will work."

"What is it?" Bryce asks.

"The spell we found will allow Kailani to choose," Celine says.

"What do you mean, choose?"

"I don't understand," I chirp out before Bran can respond, my voice rising with my stress level. "I choose to be human. Forever."

Suppressed

"And with this spell you can be," Celine says, her voice soft. "Kailani, you'll have legs and be completely human as long as you stay out of the ocean."

I feel my heart drop out of chest and land in my stomach. "And if I go into the water?"

"You'll transform into a mermaid."

"Would I be able to change back?"

My heart jumps back into my chest and beats double time. The thought of being able to swim, as a mermaid, sends excitement barreling through my body. Shooting through the water, propelled by a tail, not having to stop to breathe… it would be amazing.

"Yes," Celine says, "but isn't it dangerous for you? Bryce told us your mother's story. It is our understanding that if you become a mermaid, the merpeople *will* find you, and you'll be killed."

I feel Bryce's arm come around me as her words sink in. She's right. If this spell works, and they seem to think it will, I can never go swimming in the ocean again. If I do, I'm as good as dead. And if I don't… I can't even bear to think about it. I'm going to lose my happy place, my safe space, forever.

Shaking off the thought, I steel my spine. If I don't let them cast the spell, I'm dead. Being landlocked is better than being dead. At least, I think it is.

"When can we do the spell?"

Bran shoots me a smile. It's full of warmth and something else... pride, maybe. "The spell works best at night, under the light of the full moon."

"There's a full moon tonight," Bryce says, his arm tightening around me. "Can you get everything prepared that quickly? I don't know if Kai can last another month this way."

"That is why we made sure to be home by today," Celine says. "We have everything we need." She looks from Bryce to me. "As long as you're ready?"

My eyes dart from her to Bran to Bryce. Taking a deep breath, I give a firm nod. "I'm ready."

***

"I'd like to show you something."

Celine and I are alone in the kitchen. Bryce and his dad are down at the beach making preparations for tonight. The spell ritual will begin at midnight when the moon reaches its highest point in the sky, only eight hours from now.

"Sure," I say, following her as she leads me to the staircase.

"After we moved in," she says over her shoulder as we climb the stairs, "I spent some time exploring the house and found some things in the attic I think you should see."

Opening a door at the end of the hall, she stands aside and motions for me to precede her up the wooden stairs on the other side. I see a switch on the wall just inside and flick it up. Light from a single, bare bulb brightens the narrow staircase. I take the steps slowly, each one creaking loudly under my weight.

When we reach the top, Celine leans past me and hits another switch. Long, fluorescent bulbs flicker to life, bringing light to the dark shadows of the space. Celine steps forward, and I follow her across the long, narrow room until she stops in front of a tall object covered by a dusty, white sheet.

"I wasn't being completely truthful earlier when we were talking about your hair," she says, clasping her hands together. "I have seen that color before."

"Okay," I say, unsure of where this is going.

"I didn't know until today that your family used to live here. Bryce told me earlier and suddenly this made sense."

"What made sense?"

Without answering, she grabs the sheet and gives it a hard tug. It billows down, the dust causing my already dry throat to close up. I bend over and cough until tears burn my eyes, attempting to pull some clean air into my lungs.

"I'm sorry, Dear," Celine says, patting my firmly on the back. "I wasn't thinking."

I look up to respond, to tell her it's okay, but the words die on my lips as my eyes land on the large painting she uncovered. My mother, standing barefoot in the sand with the ocean behind her. My father, one arm wrapped around her waist and pulling her in close, the other arm holding a toddler with fiery red hair put up in pigtails.

"That's me," I say, rubbing a fingertip across the canvas. "And my mom… and dad."

Suppressed

"Yes, I assumed so after Bryce told me this was your family home."

Scrubbing the back of my hand across my eyes, I sniff loudly. "Sorry. You know, dust."

"Kai... is it all right if I call you Kai?" At my nod, she continues, "Kai, I know how important you are to my son. I want you to know that you are important to me and to Bran as well. We want you to consider this your home and if, I mean when your mother comes back it will be her home again too."

The tears I'd been straining to hold back burst free at her words. "Y-you-you'll use the spell on her too?" I stutter out.

Celine's arms wrap tight around me. "Of course, Darling. Of course, we will."

"Thank you," I whisper, pulling from her embrace. "I don't know how I'll ever repay you for everything."

"There's no need to repay us, Kai. We would do anything for our son. We're happy to help." She turns and opens the lid of a wooden trunk on the floor beside her. "Now, here's the other thing I wanted to show you."

Reaching inside, she gently lifts out a swath of green fabric. With a flick of her wrist, it unfolds and floats toward the floor. With tiny spaghetti straps pinched between her fingers, Celine holds the dress in front of her body.

"It's beautiful," I say admiring the forest green chiffon. "Wait." I look from the dress, to the painting and back to the dress again. "Is this the same one?"

Celine nods, holding the dress against my body. "Looks like it might fit," she says. "I think you should wear this tonight."

"I don't know…"

"You must," she says when I trail off. "Your mother would want you to have it. You are going to look so beautiful, ready to start the next phase of your life."

"Thank you."

I can't think of anything else to say. As I run my hand over the silky material, I look back at the painting. We all look so happy. One day, we'll be together and happy like that again. I have to believe it will happen. No matter what it takes, I *will* get my family back.

Suppressed

"I think I..."

My words trail off as I look left to right, scanning the attic. I'm alone.

"I think I will wear it," I whisper to the empty room, "for my mother."

Wendi L. Wilson

Chapter 29

"Wow."

I can't stop my lips from curving upward. The hem of my mother's dress tickles the tops of my bare feet as I twirl around for Bryce's inspection. Laughter bubbles up from my chest at the sight of his slack mouth and glossy eyes.

"Stop it," I say, slapping his arm. "It's just a dress."

"Kai, you look beautiful." I turn my head toward the voice where Celine is standing in the doorway leading from the kitchen. She glides across the carpeted floor toward us and puts her arm around Bryce. "That is what my son is trying to say," she adds with a grin.

"Okay, everything down at the beach is ready. Oh, wow," Bran says as he enters the living room from the deck.

Tinkling laughter spills from Celine's mouth. "Ah, the Howell men and their way with words. How is a girl ever to resist?"

Warmth fills me as I look from one face to the next. "Thank you all so much. I don't know what I would do without you."

Bryce snaps himself out of his stupor and clasps both of my hands in his. "You'll never have to find out."

Pain sears through my head, and a groan escapes my lips before I can stop it. I ignored the dull throb while I was getting dressed and straightening my hair. I can't ignore it anymore. I pull my hands from Bryce's and massage my temples as I stumble to the couch.

"Here. Drink this."

I crack my eyes open and look at Celine, who is standing in front of me. She takes my hand and presses a cool glass filled with red liquid into it. I press it to my lips and take a large swig. Turning my head to the side, I spew it out across the leather sofa.

"Ugh," I say, fighting the urge to spit. "It's salty."

"Sorry, dear. I should have warned you. It's purified water mixed with sea salt and electrolyte powder. I think it will help more than plain water since what your body really needs is to be in the ocean."

"I'm sorry," I say as Bran pulls a handkerchief from his pocket and mops up the red fluid from the couch.

"Don't worry about it," he says. "See? Good as new."

Fresh pain sears through my head, and I nearly drop the glass. Keeping a tight grip on it, I toss it back and gulp it down in three large swallows. Immediately, the pain starts to recede and my body feels energized.

"Woah. That's amazing."

"Feel better?" Celine asks, taking the empty glass from my hand.

"Much better, thanks."

"Good," she says, taking Bran's hand. "We have a few things to finish up in the kitchen then we'll be ready to begin the spell." She looked up at the face of the clock on the wall. "It's eleven-thirty. We'll meet you on the beach in twenty minutes, okay?"

"Okay," I say, watching them leave the room.

"Do you really feel better?" Bryce asks, sitting down next to me and pulling me against his chest.

"I really do. I wish we would have thought of that before."

"Yeah, me too." He brushes a hand down my hair. "You really do look amazing."

"Thanks."

"Did you talk to Ana?"

"I did. She wanted to come, but I told her to stay home. I didn't know how your parents would feel performing magic in front of a stranger, especially after training you your whole life to keep it a secret. Do they know that we told her?"

"Yes," he says, sighing. "They weren't too happy about it, but what's done is done. I think I convinced them we can trust her."

After a few beats of silence I pull away from him so I can look into his eyes. "So... this is it."

The corners of his mouth lift a little. "Yep. This is it."

"What if it doesn't work?" I whisper.

Suppressed

"It will work," he says, leaning forward and brushing his lips against mine. "It has to."

"Will you take a walk with me? I feel like I need to clear my head and maybe dip my toes in the water."

"Of course," he says, standing and pulling me to my feet. "Anything you need. Always."

The anxiety gripping my chest eases as soon as my feet hit the sand. The warmth of Bryce's hand in mine comforts me further. We walk straight down to the waterline, the frothy water chilling my bare toes, energizing me further. I feel the sea calling to me, begging me to submerge myself, but I ignore it. With Bryce leading the way we turn right, strolling along the shoreline.

"Well, isn't this just so ro*man*tic?"

The snide voice stops me in my tracks. Releasing Bryce's hand, I whip around and stumble back a few steps. Fear seizes my heart. Old fear that has lived inside me since I was a small child. New fear that developed only recently, when she revealed her true nature and destroyed my life.

"Coraline."

The word slips from my mouth, unbidden. Unease fills me, and not even the sea water swirling around my feet can relieve it. She materialized right here, right now, for a reason. If there's one thing I know about her, it's that she never does anything without a reason. She's here to stop us. To stop the spell from happening. To stop me from becoming human. To end my life.

"I know what you are up to, Kailani."

The way she says my name sends a fresh round of shivers down my spine. It's filled with disgust. Hatred fueled with power. It robs me of my ability to respond so I just stand where I am, my breaths coming quickly through my slightly parted lips.

"It will not happen," she says, punctuating each word with a shake of her fist. "I will not allow it."

"You can't stop us."

Bryce's sudden words nearly cause me to jump out of my skin. I have been so transfixed by Ms. Coraline that I forgot he was standing beside me. My fear ratchets up a few more notches as the scene from my bedroom plays in my head. Bryce going up against her, then, with a few words and a flick of her hand, disappearing. I can't let her hurt him.

As she lifts a hand toward him, I step between them, both mine raised in a placating manner. "Please. Please Ms. Coraline. Leave him out of this. It's me you want."

Harsh laughter erupts from her mouth, causing me to flinch. "My, aren't you the conceited, self-centered girl I always knew you to be?" She shakes her head. "I couldn't care less about you. You are not the one with the power here."

I feel Bryce move into place beside me. Taking my hand in his, he squeezes my fingers hard, causing the ever-present electric tingles to spike and shoot up my arm. My head whips toward him, and he whispers something to me. One word. Three syllables. Evelyn.

I lose the ability to breath. My head whips up toward the sky. The full moon sits, large and round and shining its bright light down on us. The sound of the waves crashing on the sand fills my ears. Evelyn saw this. The beach. The full moon. She saw Bryce and I facing down this witch. Holding hands. Lightning.

This is it. "...nothing you can do." Her words float in and out of my conscious mind.

This is the moment. "I will be the end of..."

I feel the power building inside Bryce, transferring to me and back to him again. "...imperat et..."

Before she can utter the final words that would destroy us, Bryce lifts his hand, palm facing out. I grit my teeth as pain lances through me. Electricity burns across my skin, seizing my muscles, stopping my heart. An intense flash of light blinds me, and I hear a harsh scream. The rough scrape of sand against my face is the last thing I feel before everything goes black.

Chapter 30

"Kailani?"

The voice sounds muffled, like someone is trying to talk with a pillow pressed against their mouth. I try to focus on it, to pull myself from the black abyss I seem to be floating in. My face itches, a thousand little pinpricks stabbing me at once, but I can't lift my hand to rub the annoyance away. I have no control of my body.

"Kai, please. Wake up."

"Bryce."

The scratchy, whispered word forms on my lips of its own volition. Feeling returns to my body, and I crack open my eyes. His face, upside down, fills my vision. He looks scared so I reach up and touch his cheek with my fingertips.

"What happened?"

Bryce's face relaxes and relieved tears leak from his eyes. "Hey, I thought I'd lost you there."

Scrubbing a hand across my face to relive the itchy feeling, I take note of my surroundings. I'm flat on my back in the wet sand, my head resting on Bryce's knees. A sniffle draws my attention to the right. Celine fidgets from foot to foot with Bran's arm slung around her shoulders.

I sit up a little too quickly, and my vision swings out of focus. Squeezing my eyes closed, I press my palms against them until the dizziness subsides.

"What happened to me?"

"We did it," Bryce says, a grin plastered on his face. "She's gone."

"She…" Before I can finish, everything comes rushing back to me at once. Ms. Coraline, the beach, the moon… the lightning. "She's gone?"

In a flash, Bryce's arms are around me, and my face is pressed against his chest. I feel the words vibrating in his chest as he recounts everything that happened including me passing out as soon as the lightning left his palm. I pull away to look into his eyes.

"And she just… what? Disappeared into thin air?"

"Yes," he says, snapping his fingers. "Just like that."

"Where did she go?"

"I don't know and I don't care. As long as she's gone and doesn't pose a danger to you, I'm happy."

We both look over as Bran clears his throat. "I'm sorry to interrupt, but if we are going to cast the spell tonight, we need to do it now. It's almost midnight."

Standing, Bryce clasps my hands and gently pulls me to my feet. *God, I'm so glad you're okay.*

"Me too."

He scrunches his eyebrows. "What?"

"I said, 'me too'."

"You too, what?" *What the hell is wrong with her?*

"Nothing is wrong with me, Bryce." Anger rises within me. "You said you were glad I'm okay and I said, 'me too'."

"Kai." He grabs my hand, stopping me from stomping along behind his parents without him. "I didn't say that."

"Yes, you did. Why are you doing this?"

I'm not doing anything. I never said that. Not out loud.

I hear the words, clear as a bell. The only problem is, Bryce's lips are pressed together in a thin line. He didn't speak them. I must be going crazy.

"You're not going crazy," he says.

I take a quick step back, flinching at his words. "How did you...? Did I...? What is happening, Bryce?"

"Everything okay?" Bran says, coming back to check on us. "We really need to get this spell started."

"Dad," Bryce says, pausing for a second as if to collect his thoughts, "Kai and I can read each other's minds."

"Yes, you told me she can project thoughts to you. And your ability is enhanced with her due to your synergy."

"No," I say, my head shaking back and forth. "This isn't the same. I can hear his thoughts, as if he's speaking directly to me."

"And I can hear hers."

Bran rocks back on his heels in the sand. "The diviner said something like this might happen."

Suppressed

"And you didn't tell us?" Bryce asks, his voice demanding.

"Now, son, Evelyn didn't tell me anything specific. She just said your bond would intensify if you use the physical manifestation." He puts a palm up and lunges forward, mimicking Bryce's use of the lightning bolt. "She said it would tie you together, even tighter than before."

The steam blows out of Bryce and, with sagging shoulders, he looks at me. "Are you okay with this?"

Looking at him, feeling all the love and devotion between us, I know the answer to that. I am okay with it. I'm more than okay. It's going to be awkward at times, like with the whole shower incident. But I'll take awkward any day if it means being more closely bonded with Bryce. My soulmate.

I feel the same way. His smile is huge, that real smile that he devotes solely to me.

"Bryce? Kai?" his mother calls from down the beach. "Come quickly! We have to do this now."

Sand kicks up, spread in every direction from our feet as we sprint across the beach. We come to a skidding halt when we reach Celine with Bran just a few steps behind us. My mouth drops open at the sight before me.

Fat, white candles, set in a large circle in the sand, flicker in the wind. Strange symbols ring the inside. I look closer, trying to discern what they are, but they look like hieroglyphics to me. I have no idea what they mean.

"You need to step inside the circle, Kai," Celine says, motioning me to a spot where there is a break in the line. "I'll close it after you enter."

My nerves ratchet up a few notches now that the time has come to do this. What if it doesn't work? What if I turn into a mermaid and have to go into the sea?

It's going to work.

Bryce's thought fills my head as he takes my hand. I can hear him chanting in his head, sending calming waves into my body through the physical connection. Can he do that without touching me now? Because of our bond?

"We'll try it later," he whispers, nudging me closer to the circle.

Suppressed

With one last reassuring squeeze, he releases my hand. Taking a deep breath, I lift my foot to step inside the circle. Celine and Bran are already chanting, their comforting voices complimenting the sound of the waves breaking nearby. As my foot touches the sand, a keening wail pounds against my eardrums. Using my palms to muffle the sound, I stumble back.

"Kailani Ericson, daughter to Merryn of Delmare and the human, Dante Ericson, I come with a message from our king."

My eyes scan the water frantically, looking for the source of the voice. The waves shift, and I see him about thirty yards out. With the moon reflecting its brilliant light off of his platinum blond hair and pale, muscular torso, he's hard to miss.

"Our king holds your father and your mother in his custody. Our king decrees that you shall come to Delmare and face punishment for being the abomination that you are. You have one day to get your affairs in order. Tomorrow night, when the moon is at its zenith, I will come back and escort you to your fate. If you refuse, your parents will be executed."

Just as suddenly as he appeared, he's gone. The roar of the ocean returns in full force, making me realize that it had somehow been muted while the man... merman... whatever he calls himself had been speaking. Tears sting my eyes as I replay his words over and over in my mind.

"Kai, get in the circle," Bryce says, his urgent voice breaking through my thoughts.

"What?" I ask lamely.

"Get in. We have to do the spell. We're running out of time. We'll figure out the rest later."

I take a step in the wrong direction. "I'm sorry, Bryce."

"Kai, don't. We will figure this out together. Just get in the circle."

"I have to save them." *I'm sorry. I love you,* I add mentally. Without looking back, I dash toward the water. Toward my parents. Toward my destiny.

Thank you for reading Suppressed. I really hope you enjoyed it! If you have time, it would really help me out if you could leave a review.

Thank you so much!

Sign up for my newsletter to get news and info on new releases!
http://wendilwilson.wixsite.com/author

Wendi L. Wilson

Suppressed

Wendi L. Wilson

Made in United States
Orlando, FL
22 February 2022